C0-DAM-492

The beast had its back turned to the Gunsmith, but it seemed to stiffen at the sound of Clint's voice. It slowly rose to full height. Clint's mouth fell open as he realized the beast was more than seven feet tall.

Suddenly, the thing bolted. Clint watched the big brown shape run into the forest. Clint thought, *Nothing that big can move that fast; but this thing runs on its hind legs like a man!*

Don't miss any of the lusty, hard-riding action in the new Charter Western series, THE GUNSMITH:

And coming next month:

# THE GUNSMITH

## 21

### SASQUATCH HUNT

J.R. ROBERTS

CHARTER BOOKS, NEW YORK

All characters in this book are fictitious.
Any resemblance to actual persons, living or dead,
is purely coincidental.

THE GUNSMITH #21: SASQUATCH HUNT

A Charter Book/published by arrangement with the author

PRINTING HISTORY
Charter Original/October 1983

All rights reserved.
Copyright © 1983 by Robert J. Randisi
This book may not be reproduced in whole
or in part, by mimeograph or any other means,
without permission. For information address:
The Berkley Publishing Group,
200 Madison Avenue, New York, N.Y. 10016

ISBN: 0-441-30892-9

Charter Books are published by The Berkley Publishing Group,
200 Madison Avenue, New York, N.Y. 10016.
PRINTED IN THE UNITED STATES OF AMERICA

*Dedicated to Stacy Varon*

# SASQUATCH HUNT

# ONE

"You're the Gunsmith?" Sheriff Walter Sloan asked, staring at the tall, slender stranger who'd just entered his office.

"That's what some folks call me," Clint Adams confessed with a sigh.

Sloan glanced over the supposed living legend. Clint's denim shirt and Levi's were coated with trail dust. He could have been mistaken for a saddle bum unless one noticed the clean, well-oiled .45-caliber Colt revolver in a holster hung low on his right hip.

"Always figured you'd look different," Sloan remarked. Nothing about the Gunsmith suggested he was a hardcase except for the way he wore his gun and the long jagged scar on his left cheek which marred an otherwise handsome face.

"Sorry." Clint grinned. "I'm what you get."

"Well"—the sheriff shrugged—"what do you want, mister?"

"You can call me Clint, Sheriff. And I just stopped by to let you know I'm in town. Used to be a lawman myself, so I know a fella who wears a badge always likes to know about strangers with . . . a reputation who happen to be in his jurisdiction."

"So you're warning me, eh?" Sloan's eyes narrowed.

1

"Just the opposite," the Gunsmith assured him. "I'm letting you know I'm here so it doesn't come as a surprise later."

"What's your business here, Adams?"

"I'm a gunsmith," Clint explained. "You might have heard that a newspaper man labeled me 'The Gunsmith' when I was still a deputy sheriff in Oklahoma, but I make my living as a gunsmith now."

"How long were you a lawman, Adams?" Sloan asked as he got out a pouch of tobacco and rolling papers.

"Eighteen years," Clint answered.

"Why'd you quit wearin' a badge?"

"Personal reasons."

"Other kinds of work pay better, I reckon," Sloan commented, rolling a cigarette. "You make much money as a gunsmith, Adams?"

"Enough," Clint told him.

"I heard you make a lot of money by using that gun of yours," the sheriff said as he struck a match on the top of his battered old desk. "Some say you're supposed to be the fastest gun around. Folks figure only man who mighta been as fast and accurate with a gun as you, was Wild Bill Hickok. 'Course he's dead now. Way I hear it, you and him was supposed to be friends anyway."

"You heard right."

"But you say you're not a pistolman?" Sloan asked, puffing on his cigarette.

"I don't make my living that way," the Gunsmith insisted.

"But you still gunned down Con Macklin, Parako, that Chinaman they called the Dragon Kid, Stansfield Lloyd and that crippled marshal in Palmerville. He sorta went crazy after he lost his arm, least that's what a feller who'd spent some time up in Wyoming around 'seventy-four told me. All those men was supposed to be pretty good with a gun."

"And none of them gave me any other choice except to defend myself." Clint's temper slowly was reaching the boiling point.

"Now, why'd you say you was in my town?" Sloan asked.

"I haven't told you yet," Clint replied. "And if you're just going to sit there and act like a suspicious shit, I'm not going to waste my time talking to you, Sheriff."

"All right." Sloan sighed. "You ain't a wanted man, so I've got no reason to figure you're looking for trouble."

Clint nodded. "I'm a gunsmith. I make my living by traveling from town to town with my wagon and offering my services—*as a gunsmith*. That's why I'm here."

"You bring that big black Arabian gelding with you?"

"Duke's my partner," the Gunsmith replied. "Anywhere I go, he goes."

"Heard he's quite a horse," the sheriff remarked.

"You heard right about that," the Gunsmith confirmed.

"How long you figure on being in town?"

"Only for a day or two," Clint answered. "Talo isn't big enough to have many customers for a gunsmith, so I won't stay very long. There are plenty of other places in California that offer a hell of a lot more business for a man in my line of work."

"You spend much time in California, Adams?"

"Some," Clint replied. "I've never been this far north in the state before."

"Well," the sheriff began, dropping his cigarette to the floor and grinding it under a boot heel, "just see to it you don't get in any trouble while you're in my town, Adams."

"I don't plan to be here long enough to get in any trouble, Sheriff," Clint told him. "And I doubt that I'll want to extend my visit in Talo."

"No offense, Adams," Sloan said. "But I won't be sorry to see you go."

"That'll make two of us, Sheriff," the Gunsmith muttered as he headed for the door.

# TWO

Clint took his wagon and horses to the local livery stable. He paid the hostler five dollars to take care of his rig and team—and especially Duke. When the Gunsmith was certain his wagon and animals would be safe, he headed for the only tavern in town, the Two Star Saloon.

Pushing through the batwings, the Gunsmith stared at the familiar sight of a frontier barroom. The furniture was simple and practical, wooden tables surrounded by straight-backed chairs. A cracked mirror and a weary bartender were behind the counter. Several customers sat at the tables, playing poker for matchsticks and drinking pitchers of beer. Two cowboys, covered with trail dust, stood at the bar, sharing a bottle of red-eye.

Clint strode across the sawdust-laced floor and ordered a beer. The bartender's dour expression seemed to suggest he found the request a great burden, but he bravely nodded and drew a draft from the keg.

"Much obliged," Clint told him.

"You ain't tasted it yet," a young cowboy, with a shock of blond hair dangling beneath his stetson to his forehead, remarked. "Whiskey ain't much better neither."

"If'n yore thirsty enough, it'll do," the bartender said defensively.

"Well, I'm pretty thirsty," the Gunsmith replied, sipping his brew. He was inclined to agree with the cowboy. The beer was warm and flat.

"Ain't got no ice chest," the bartender stated. "Can't expect cold beer this time of year if'n a feller don't have no icebox."

"I'm not complaining, friend," Clint assured him as he placed a silver eagle on the counter.

"Beer's a nickel, mister," the barman said. "I've had me a slow day. Ain't sure I got enough change for that there dollar."

"And ol' Bart ain't sure if'n he can count out ninety-five cents correct," the young cowpoke said with a chuckle.

"Don't you sass me, Nick Stevens." The bartender glared at him. "I've still got enough sand to throw yore ass outta here, sonny!"

"Okay, Bart," Stevens said, holding up his arms in mock surrender. "Didn't mean to get you all riled up."

"Funnin' folks is just Nick's way," the other cowhand, older and quieter than his friend, added. "No need to get in a huff, Bart."

"Bart," Clint began, "here's a nickel, but you're welcome to keep that dollar if you'll do me a favor."

"What sorta favor you askin' for, mister?" Bart gazed suspiciously at the Gunsmith.

"I'm going to be in town for a day or two. I'm a gunsmith by trade and I'd appreciate all the business I can get. If you know anybody who needs repairs or modifications done on his firearms, you might suggest they pay me a visit. Got my tools and such in my wagon over at the livery, but—"

"A traveling gunsmith?" Nick Stevens interrupted, staring at Clint as if he'd claimed he was an alchemist who could change lead into gold. "You mean you're Clint Adams? *The* Gunsmith?"

"That's a fact," Clint confessed. "You fellas have any firearms that need some work done on them?"

"Maybe I do at that." The young cowboy grinned.

He slowly drew a .44-caliber Army Colt from its holster and handed it, butt first, to the Gunsmith. Clint opened the loading gate and ejected the shells, one by one.

"Handing a fella a loaded pistol is a might careless, friend," he remarked. "This gun seems in pretty good shape to me. What do you want done with her, Nick?"

"Is it true that gun you're packin' fires double action?" Nick asked.

"Yeah." The Gunsmith nodded. "I modified it myself."

"Way I hear it," Nick continued, "you're quicker than a rattler with that gun, and she shoots faster than a summer lightning."

"A double-action gun doesn't have to be cocked when you fire it," Clint explained. "Since you only need to squeeze the trigger, it means you can fire faster than with a single-action revolver that has to be cocked before each shot. It isn't as accurate and it takes some time to get used to. Double action doesn't make it any faster on the draw. That's something that just requires plenty of practice to acquire."

"Can you modify my Colt to fire double action?" Nick asked eagerly.

"That'd take a whole lot of work, friend," Clint answered. "And I'd have to charge you quite a bit for parts, time and labor. It took me a couple years before I finally converted my Colt to fire double action. Hell, I had to rebuild and modify more than half the parts before I got it right. Starr has a double-action Army forty-four on the market, but I haven't heard anything good about its performance. The new Smith & Wesson Schofield model forty-five could be converted to fire double action without too much work.''

Nick frowned. ''You say quick draw takes a lot of practice. What else should I do? File down the front sight or put in a trigger shoe?''

''Don't file off the front sight unless you don't give a damn about accuracy,'' Clint warned. ''Some fellas do that because they want to prevent the sight from snagging on leather when they draw. It's a better idea to get a holster designed for a fast draw and made for the gun you carry instead. Trigger shoes are an even worse idea because they extend beyond the trigger guard.''

''That's what makes 'em easier to fire,'' Nick insisted. ''Faster too . . .''

''Maybe that's what somebody claimed in the *Police Gazette* or wherever you found out about trigger shoes,'' Clint said. ''Fact is, the shoe can actually slip out of place and jam the trigger. Worse, it can even catch on leather when you holster the gun. You're not going to be much of a pistolman if you start your reputation as the man who shot himself in the foot.''

''I didn't say I was lookin' to be a pistolman,'' Nick replied.

''Yes, you did. The questions you've been asking make your intentions clear enough. I'll give you some more advice—don't try to get famous by using a gun.''

''You've done all right, Mr. Adams.''

''Call me Clint, and I *haven't* done all right. I've got a reputation I never wanted but can't get rid of unless someone puts a bullet in me. I've always got to watch out for old enemies and snot-nosed kids looking for a rep. If you want to be famous, you'd better find another way.''

"Thanks for the sermon, Clint," Nick said with a sneer. Then he turned and marched to the door.

"I've been givin' him that same advice for almost a year now," the other cowboy sighed. "I hope you made a better impression than I did, Clint."

"So do I," the Gunsmith said, watching Nick Stevens push through the batwings.

Another man was coming in just then and bumped shoulders with Stevens. The newcomer, a tall man with a gray scrub-brush mustache and long mutton-chops on his cheeks, was dressed in a tweed suit with a cloth cap perched on his head. He touched the brim of his hat, about to apologize to Nick, but Stevens angrily shoved him aside and stomped out of the saloon.

"That's not typical of western hospitality, friend," Clint told the stranger clad in the eastern suit. "Since I put that fella in a foul mood, I'd be glad to make amends by buying you a drink."

"Oh, that's terribly decent of you, sir," the man replied, revealing a strong British accent. "Thank you."

"Clint," the cowboy put in, "since Nick is my buddy, I'd be obliged if'n you'd let me buy this round."

"And I'll be pleased to accept," the Gunsmith answered. "Providing you let me pay for the next one."

"My mama didn't raise no stupid children." The cowhand grinned. "Name's Jed Stark."

"Pleasure to meet you, Jed," Clint declared, shaking his hand.

"I'm Edward Wardell," the Englishman told them. "Doctor Wardell, actually, but don't ask me for medical advice because I'm not that sort of doctor. I'm an archaeologist at the British Museum in London.''

"What's an archy-ologist?'' Jed asked.

"An archaeologist is a chap who digs about in old ruins and such looking for relics and fossils that might help us learn more about man's past,'' Wardell answered.

"Oh.'' Jed nodded. "That's what I thought it was.''

"You're a long way from home, Doctor,'' the Gunsmith remarked as he shook the Briton's hand.

"Don't I know it. Of course, my profession does have me hopping about from country to country. Get to see a bit of the world, so it's not so bad really.''

"I move around some myself,'' Clint remarked.

"Say, what was wrong with that rude chap I bumped into? Overreacted a bit, didn't he?''

"Fella wants to be a gunfighter when he grows up,'' Clint answered. "I just told him the facts of life and he didn't care for what he heard.''

"What'll you gents have?'' the bartender asked. He didn't seem any happier now that business had picked up than he had been when it was too slow.

"Have you any brandy?'' Wardell inquired.

"You tryin' to be cute, feller?'' the barman replied sharply.

"We'll take three shots of red-eye, Bart,'' Jed Stark ordered. He turned to Clint and Wardell. "Trust me.''

"It can't be any worse than the beer.'' The Gunsmith shrugged.

"Try to excuse Nick,'' Jed told Wardell, tilting his head toward the batwings. "He's young and eager to make somethin' of hisself. Reckons he won't manage by being a cowpuncher all his life—and I can't say as I can argue with that."

"Quite all right," the Briton assured him. "We all get a bit nasty from time to time, I suppose."

"Thirty cents," Bart announced, filling three shot glasses with amber liquid.

Stark paid him. The Gunsmith sipped his drink and decided the red-eye wasn't much better than the watered-down, flat beer, but at least it tasted like whiskey.

"Perhaps you chaps can help me," Wardell began. "You see, I'm looking for someone to hire as a guide. I've not the foggiest notion about what the forests around these parts are like and I rather need someone who does."

"You here on a huntin' trip, Doc?" Jed asked.

"You might say that," the Briton nodded.

"Plenty of game in these parts," Stark told him. "If you know where to look. Injuns 'round here are pretty tame. Shasta, Wintu and Huppa mostly. Maybe a few Moduc that drifted down from Oregon. Not real dangerous in them woods unless you happen to cross a grizzly or a pack of wolves and you do somethin' stupid to get 'em mad at you."

"Oh," Wardell replied, "I think there's a good chance it could get a bit dangerous. I'd rather like my guide to be skilled with a gun as well, just in case."

"Well"—Stark sighed—"I don't know who you could hire who'd be both guide and troubleshooter, but—"

"Adams!" a voice shouted from the batwings.

Clint turned to see two men enter the Two Star Saloon. Both were over six feet tall, heavy boned and thickly muscled. Their clothes were stained with dirt and trail dust and their boots splattered with mud. One fellow wore a beard and the other sported a mustache.

They stood side by side, their feet spread shoulder-width apart, hands draped over the grips of pistols worn in hip holsters. They seemed eager to use their six-guns and there was no mistaking the fierce, hateful expressions on their faces. Their teeth were clenched in anger and killers' lust reflected in their eyes.

The two men strongly resembled one another, and Clint was sure he had seen that face before—not just the same expression. But it had been years ago and Clint couldn't put a name to the vaguely remembered face.

"You killed our brother, Adams!" the man with the beard snarled.

Patrons in the saloon scrambled out of the line of fire. Jed Stark grabbed Wardell's sleeve and towed him out of the way while Bart ducked down behind his bar.

"Is that a fact?" Clint mused, still holding a shot class in his left hand while his right fell to the well-oiled, modified Colt on his hip.

"Yeah," the bearded man answered.

"Did your brother have a name?" Clint asked.

"Ron Shagan," the one with the mustache replied.

"Shagan?" Clint frowned. "Name seems familiar . . ."

"Baxterville, Missouri," the bearded brother supplied. "Used to be called Macklinville. Remember?"

"Oh, yeah." Clint nodded. "I remember Shagan now. I broke a chair over his thick skull to teach him some manners. Your brother liked to beat up women. . . ."

"They was Con Macklin's sluts!" the other brother snapped. "Them whores deserved whatever bad happened to them."

"So did your brother," the Gunsmith said. "Figure I ought to let you fellas know that Shagan had two other fellas with him when he made his final play against me after I left Baxterville. He and his friends shouldn't have followed me. You two shouldn't have either."

"You expect us to turn around and crawl outta here?" the bearded man said with a snicker.

"Just as soon you didn't," Clint told him. "You two are bound to keep on tracking me and I'd have to kill you sooner or later. May as well make it now."

The pair stiffened, their eyes betraying fear, but they held their ground.

"One question," the Gunsmith began. "How'd you know your brother was dead?"

"His body was found on the shore of the river where you dumped him," the Shagan with the mustache explained.

"Must not have weighted him down with enough rocks." Clint sighed. "Still, I wasn't about to wear myself out digging a grave for scum like—"

The two Shagan brothers made their move together. They'd obviously rehearsed the technique. The Shagans figured if they both drew at the same time, their opponent would be too startled by multiple targets and hesitate before he'd shoot. The method gave the brothers a definite edge in a gunfight. Even if one Shagan caught a bullet, the other had an excellent chance of hitting their adversary.

The trick would have worked against most men— even most professional gunmen—but Clint Adams was a professional's professional with a six-gun. His modified Colt appeared in his hand so fast no one even saw the blur of his arm. The pistol bellowed twice. Flame spat from the muzzle and each Shagan brother received one .45-caliber bullet in the chest.

The bearded brother staggered backward, toward the batwings. His fist was still clenched around the butt of his revolver, which was still in his holster. Clint's pistol barked again. The .45 round hit Shagan in the chest, left of center. The big hairy man hurtled through the saloon doors to fall in a dying heap outside.

No one could accuse the Shagans of being ninety-eight pound weaklings. The brother with the mustache had stumbled into a table and knocked over a pitcher of beer, a deck of cards and about five hundred matchsticks. His sternum had been shattered by Clint's bullet, but he was still on his feet.

The Gunsmith fired once more. A bullet ripped through Shagan's forehead. The big man's body seemed to hop backward as if eager to make contact with the window behind him. Glass and framework exploded and the second Shagan brother crashed to the plankwalk—dead.

Onlookers gasped in awe, glancing through the broken window at the lifeless Shagans and then at Clint Adams. The Gunsmith still held the shot glass in his left hand. He hadn't spilled a drop during the entire confrontation. Clint raised it to his lips and gulped the whiskey down.

"What in hell is going on here?" Sheriff Walt Sloan demanded as he entered the saloon.

"Not much." The Gunsmith shrugged. "I just set-tled a family argument."

# THREE

Sheriff Sloan wasn't amused by Clint's remark, but plenty of witnesses to the shooting confirmed that the Gunsmith had acted in self-defense. This seemed to disappoint the lawman. Sloan glared at Clint Adams as he approached.

"I thought you said you was here to fix guns," he growled. "Not to get in gunfights yourself."

"They came looking for me, Sheriff," Clint replied. "Not the other way around. Would you feel better if I'd just stood still and let them shoot me instead?"

Sloan shrugged as if to say yes.

"Jesus," Nick Stevens remarked as he entered the Two Star. "You kill these fellers, Clint?"

"They didn't die from mosquito bites, mister," Sloan muttered sourly.

"They draw on you, Clint?" the young cowpoke inquired.

"I don't kill men for fun," the Gunsmith told him.

"Why'd they call you out?" Nick asked.

"Because of something that happened years ago," Clint answered. "That's what you can expect when you have a reputation, kid. Total strangers come looking to kill you."

"I never thought of it that way before," Nick admitted, gazing out the shattered window at the blood-stained, faceless body sprawled across the plankwalk.

A crowd had gathered around the Two Star Saloon. They gaped at the corpses of the Shagan brothers as they chattered away about the remarkable shooting by the Gunsmith. Some noticed the accuracy of Clint's bullet placement in the dead men's bodies. Others pointed at the Shagans' pistols, which had never cleared leather before they received their .45-caliber tickets to Boot Hill. A couple of women complained about the horror of a gunfight in their nice quiet little town. The ladies still stared at the corpses and Clint Adams with fascination. One of them smiled at the Gunsmith.

"Okay," Sheriff Sloan snapped as he stormed outside to shoo away the rubberneckers. "It's all over now. Some drifters got in a gun brawl. No locals involved, so you can all go home. Get!"

"I must say," Wardell began, stepping next to Clint, "that was an incredible display of marksmanship."

"Better them than me," Clint muttered as he removed four spent cartridge casings from his modified Colt and replaced them with fresh shells. "If you fellas don't mind, I'll pay for your round, but I'll have to join you some other time. I'd sort of like to get myself settled in at the hotel now."

"Oh, well"—the Briton followed Clint to the batwings—"I'd like to make you an offer. . . ."

"I'm not for hire," Clint told him. "As a guide or a gunman."

The Gunsmith pushed through the batwings. Bart cried out, "Hey! What about my window?"

"The fella who broke it is lying on the plankwalk,"

Clint replied. "Check his pockets and see if he can pay for the damages. If he doesn't have enough cash, see if his brother can cover the rest. I don't reckon they'll mind much."

Clint signed the register at the only hotel in Lincoln and headed back to the livery to see how his wagon and horses were. The hostler had followed Clint's instructions and taken good care of the rig and animals. He spent fifteen minutes with Duke, his prize Arabian gelding. Clint brushed the animal's glossy black coat, talked to him for a while and made certain Duke was comfortable before he left.

The Gunsmith returned to the hotel with saddlebags draped over his shoulder and a Springfield .45 carbine in his fist. He mounted the stairs to the second floor, located his room and seized the doorknob as he tucked the rifle under his arm and prepared to insert a key into the lock.

The doorknob turned in his hand and the door creaked open.

Clint reacted immediately. He dropped to one knee by the side of the doorway and drew his revolver as he cautiously pushed the door open. Keeping low, presenting as small a target as possible, Clint thrust the Colt barrel into the room.

A tall, beautiful blonde stood in the middle of the room—stark naked. Clint stared at her slender, yet shapely body. The woman's honey blond hair framed a lovely oval face with fair skin and big blue eyes. Her breasts were large with pert pink nipples; her waist was trim, the lean curves of her hips extending to superb, long legs.

"You've got a hell of a way of greeting a girl,

Clint," she remarked with a grin.

"Jenny?" the Gunsmith whispered, wondering if the rotgut whiskey he'd consumed in the Two Star Saloon was causing him to hallucinate.

"Glad you remember me, Clint," the girl replied.

Clint had met Jenny Parker about a year before. He'd been involved in an adventure that had started in Brownsville, Texas, which revolved around a fortune in gold, stolen from Mexico's National Treasury. A group of American outlaws and a gang of Mexican *bandidos* had been competing for the loot—with Clint Adams in the middle.

The Gunsmith first saw Jenny exactly as she appeared now in his hotel room—naked. Clint had saved her from four *bandidos* in her husband's farmhouse in the Arizona Territory near Yuma, and Jenny had given him some badly needed aid and comfort . . . fantastic comfort.

"Surprised to see me?" Jenny asked with a smile.

"How the hell did you get in here?" he demanded as he entered the room and closed the door.

"I'm staying with my sister's family here in Talo," Jenny replied. "Her husband owns the general store across the street. I saw you leave the saloon after the shooting and head for the hotel. So I sneaked in through the side door and checked the register when the desk clerk wasn't looking. Then I just came up here to your room and waited for you to return. Thought I'd surprise you."

"You damn well succeeded," the Gunsmith told her.

Jenny frowned. "I sort of hoped you'd be glad to see me again."

"What if your husband hears about this?" Clint

asked, trying not to look at her beautiful, naked body.

"Arnold's dead—" Jenny began.

"Oh, not again!" Clint groaned. "You told me that fairy tale the last time. Then you kicked me off your property before hubby got home."

"It wasn't quite that way, Clint."

"Pretty close." Clint couldn't stop his gaze from wandering over Jenny's magnificent body. Although he tried to resist, the Gunsmith felt his groin stir with desire.

"This time I'm telling you the truth, Clint," Jenny said grimly. "Arnold was killed in an Apache raid a few months ago. That's why I'm staying here with Annie and her family."

The Gunsmith gazed into her clear blue eyes and found no deceit in them—only pain. "I'm sorry, Jenny."

"Well, I sold the farm at a public auction in Yuma. The Apaches burned down the house and the barn and took what livestock we had, so all I had left to sell was the land. Still, I got enough money to come here."

"Do you plan to stay in Talo?" Clint asked.

"No," Jenny replied. "I'll probably head to San Francisco and try to find a job there. Not much future in this place."

"Maybe not," Clint said.

He had a photographic memory when it came to beautiful women. He'd had many women before and since Jenny Parker, yet he recalled the sexual skills of each lover vividly. Jenny had been one of the best, so it wasn't easy for him to say what he felt he had to.

"There's no future with me either."

"There may be no future with you, Clint," she admitted, "but there is a present. Right here and now, and that's all I'm concerned with. I need a man like you to make that present a little less lonely.''

The Gunsmith took her in his arms. Jenny embraced him and their lips met in a passionate kiss. Clint's hands slowly stroked the bare flesh at her shoulders and back while Jenny began to unbutton his shirt. Her fingernails gently raked the thick hair on Clint's chest. His hands tenderly fondled her breasts. He kissed her neck and gradually moved his lips lower to her nipples.

He broke the embrace to unbuckle his gunbelt and drape it over the headboard of the bed. Jenny sat on the mattress and watched the Gunsmith disrobe. She placed a hand to her tawny crotch as she gazed at his leanly muscled physique. The Gunsmith had acquired an extra scar or two since they'd last made love, yet she found his body more exciting than before. Her hand moved faster as he removed the final garments.

Clint climbed into bed with Jenny. They kissed and caressed, their mutual passion boiling hot and about to go out of control. Jenny's fingers found the Gunsmith's hard penis. She still had the same masterful touch that he'd recalled so vividly from their time together in Arizona. Clint lay on his back as she rubbed her fingertips up and down the length of his shaft. Soon his cock was throbbing in her grasp.

The Gunsmith's lust was driving him passionately berserk. Jenny straddled him, spreading her legs wide as she mounted him. Clint's stiff member found her center of love. Jenny peeled back the lips of her womb with one hand and guided his maleness with the other. The Gunsmith sighed with pleasure as he slid into the warm, moist sheath.

Jenny squirmed, working Clint's penis deeper. She

began to rock her body gently, humming her contentment. The Gunsmith resisted an urge to thrust fast and hard to satisfy his own yearning. He always considered his lover's fulfillment to be as important as his own, so he held back.

However, Jenny didn't do likewise. She began to raise and lower herself, groaning with ecstasy. Clint stared up at the ceiling and tried to let his mind go blank for a minute or two to avoid coming before Jenny approached her limit.

When she increased the tempo of her motion and began bouncing up and down vigorously, Clint assumed a more active role. He fondled her marvelous breasts, thumbing the erect nipples gently. Clint arched his back to drive himself deeper inside her cavern of joy. He joined the rhythm of Jenny's body as she rode his swollen manhood to utopia.

"Oh, God!" she cried out. "Oh, God, that feels so good!"

Jenny convulsed in a wild orgasm as Clint Adams reached the zenith of his sexual endurance as well. His cock exploded its seed into her love chamber. The Gunsmith groaned in gratitude and pleasure.

"I needed this, Clint," Jenny whispered, her head hung low. The long blond hair formed a veil over her face. "God, how I needed this!"

Clint parted the golden curtain and took her face in his hands. Tears streaked Jenny's cheeks as their eyes met.

"Jenny, I'll only be here for a day or two and then I'll be moving on. That's my way. You know that, don't you?"

She nodded.

"But tonight," Clint continued, "right here and now, we've got each other. I can't offer you more than that."

"I'm not asking for more than that," Jenny assured him. "Let's just make tonight the best we've ever had. The very best."

They made love again and again, until both were too exhausted to continue. Perhaps it wasn't the best, but it couldn't have been much better.

# FOUR

When Clint Adams awoke the following morning, Jenny Parker had already left. The Gunsmith was glad that she hadn't stayed. A love affair is best ended quickly with as few words and as little pain as possible.

Clint climbed out of bed, pulled on his clothes and buckled the gunbelt around his lean waist. Then he left the hotel in search of breakfast, which he found in a small diner—the only one in Talo.

After finishing his sausage and eggs, the Gunsmith poured a third cup of coffee from a porcelain pot. He glanced up to see Edward Wardell enter the diner. The Briton carried a long, double-barreled gun under his right arm as he approached Clint's table. From the urgency in Wardell's stride, the Gunsmith knew the encounter wasn't by happenstance. He had no reason to believe Wardell had come to do him harm, nor could he imagine any reason the Englishman might have to do so. Yet a man carrying a big gun and headed in his direction tended to make Clint a bit nervous. His right hand slipped under the table and fell to his holstered Colt.

"Good morning, Clint," Wardell said. "Mind if I join you?"

"I don't mind," the Gunsmith answered. "But I'm still not interested in your job offer, Doctor."

"I understand you're an expert with firearms," Wardell remarked. "Did a bit of asking about concerning you. Seems you're a rather famous man in the West, Clint. Or should I call you the Gunsmith?"

"No, you shouldn't," Clint said dryly.

"Have you ever seen one of these before?" the Englishman asked.

He handed his weapon to the Gunsmith. At first Clint thought it was a shotgun due to the side-by-side barrels. However, twin front sights and elevated, adjustable rear sights told him the gun was a rifle.

He examined the weapon with an expert's eye for detail and the appreciation of a true firearm enthusiast. The barrels were thick and heavy. The diameter of each muzzle was enormous, even bigger than a "Big Fifty" Sharps buffalo gun. Its metal had been beautifully blued and the stock was handcarved rosewood.

"It's a Parker-Hale big game rifle," Wardell explained. "Sixty caliber. You can bring down a charging elephant with that gun."

"I recognize it," Clint replied, handling the rifle in an almost reverent manner. "I read about it in a British firearms textbook that's in my wagon. Same one that gave me the idea for converting my Colt to fire double action." He grinned. "You English might be ahead of us when it comes to designing guns, but we're catching up fast. Just you wait and see."

"I've no doubt about that," Wardell agreed. "You Americans seem to have a real love affair with guns. What do you think of that Parker-Hale?"

"If I remember right," Clint began, "it has an effective range of almost nine hundred yards. More than that if a fella practices enough and maybe throats the barrels. I'm not sure about the velocity of the bullet, but I think, due to the size of the slug, it's a fairly slow round compared to a forty-four—forty Winchester. That means it may not have as much penetration, but a sixty caliber has a tremendous knock-down force. You could probably kill a whale with this thing.''

"You know more about it than I," the Briton admitted. "Guns really aren't my forte. I'm a scientist, not a marksman. An associate of mine in England, a big game hunter named David Colton, talked me into buying that rifle when he learned about my expedition here.''

"But I thought you were here on a hunting trip."

"Oh, yes," Wardell nodded. "That's true."

"Then why'd somebody have to convince you to bring a gun?" Clint asked as he prepared to return the rifle.

"How would you like to keep that gun?" the Briton inquired, avoiding Clint's question.

"Why don't you tell me what you're really looking for?" The Gunsmith's voice revealed his suspicion.

"There is a creature that inhabits the American Northwest," Wardell began. "It's rare and elusive and not terribly well known. Yet, it may well be the most important animal on the face of the earth, second only to man himself.''

"What sort of animal?" The Gunsmith frowned.

"It's called by many names throughout the world," the Briton answered. "In China it's known as *kungloo*, the Russians refer to it as *kaptar*, and the Sherpa, a tribe in Nepal, call it a *yeti*.''

"Okay, Doc." Clint smiled, amused by Wardell's taste for the dramatic. "If this animal is found in Asia, why are you looking for it here?''

"Because the same creature, or something very like it, is also found in this country and I think my chances are better here in an English-speaking country that's much more friendly toward Great Britain—at least now—than they'd be if I went mucking about in the Orient or Siberian tundra. Here, the Indians call it *sasquatch.*''

"Sasquatch?'' Clint's eyes widened. "You can't be serious.''

"Then you know about this creature?'' Wardell asked.

"I heard about it up in Canada some time ago,'' the Gunsmith answered. "The Indians up there call it sasquatch and ones around here call it different names, but whites usually call it Bigfoot. It's supposed to be some sort of hairy wild man. It depends on what tribe you talk to, but Indians think it's either a spirit of the forest or something that's half human and half animal. Makes you wonder what its parents were like, huh?''

"I take it you don't believe in the sasquatch?'' Wardell said with a sigh.

"Well, I've never seen a big hairy ape-man in the forest,'' Clint replied. "And I spend a lot of time on the trail.''

"Have you ever seen a wolverine?'' the Briton asked. "I doubt that you have, yet it lives in the American Northwest and Canada as well.''

"But apes aren't native to this country,'' the Gunsmith said. "As an archaeologist, I'd figure you'd know that.''

"Indeed.'' Wardell nodded. "Yet there are monkeys and lemurs found in South American countries.''

"Jesus,'' Clint muttered. "They've got jaguars and

crocodiles down there too, but you won't find any of them in Northern California.''

"You're an educated man, Clint," the Briton began. "I'm sure you know that the Bering Strait is all that separates Siberia and Alaska. Some believe there was once a solid bridge, either made of ice or land, which connected the two. The American Indian may well have crossed that bridge centuries ago. There are many similarities in certain Asian languages, cultures and religions with those of the Indians. Perhaps the first Americans did migrate across the Bering Strait. Maybe the sasquatch did likewise.''

"Hell, Doctor"—the Gunsmith groaned—"the sasquatch is a myth.''

"Have you such a low opinion of the Indians' intelligence and beliefs?'' Wardell demanded.

"I have a *lot* of *respect* for them,'' Clint stated firmly. "That doesn't mean I have to believe every superstitious bullshit story they come up with. If *you* want to, that's fine with me. While you're looking for the Bigfoot, you can also try to find the owl-demon, the river spirits and whatever other types of supernatural critters happen to strike your fancy.''

"Doesn't it seem odd to you that this 'legend' is found throughout the world?'' the Briton asked. "Why are stories of these great man-beasts so widespread?''

"There are people all over the world who believe in ghosts and sea monsters too.'' The Gunsmith shrugged. "You'd still have trouble convincing some folks the world isn't flat.''

"Then you insist that Bigfoot is just a figment of the Indians' imagination. A fantasy that just happens to also be found in Russia and China as well?''

"Maybe the effects of mescal, peyote and locoweed

are similar to those of opium and vodka.'' Clint grinned.

"And they all had the same hallucinations?'' Wardell scoffed. "Many archaeologists believe we're on the verge of discovering the ruins of the fabled lost cities of Troy and Jericho. Most legends, my friend, are based on facts.''

"Oh, there could be some truth to the Bigfoot tales,'' the Gunsmith agreed. "Have you ever met a mountain man? They're more or less hermits, but they know the mountains and the forests better than anyone short of God Almighty. Most mountain men are big, strong guys. They grow long hair and thick beards and they wear jackets, robes, boots and caps made of animal fur. They *look* like wild animals on two legs. A lot of them *behave* like animals too.

"Bigfoot is supposed to be sort of timid, right? Nobody ever seems to see more than a glimpse of him. Mountain men tend to avoid contact with other folks unless they want to trade furs for something they need. Bigfoot is also supposed to have a bad musky stink, isn't he? Well, you've never smelled bad until you smell a mountain man who hasn't bathed or changed his clothes for more than a year.''

"Do you think the entire sasquatch legend and the stories of the *yeti* and all the rest are simply exaggerated accounts of encounters with hermits in shaggy clothing?'' Wardell frowned.

"It makes sense to me,'' Clint replied.

"I can't believe that's all there is to the sasquatch.''

"Maybe you don't want to.'' The Gunsmith shrugged.

"I'd rather hoped you might be interested in joining us on the expedition after I explained it to you.'' The

Briton sighed. "You seem to be a man of principles and intelligence as well as an expert with guns."

"I'm sorry, Doctor," Clint said, handing him the Parker-Hale rifle. "But this isn't the sort of thing I care to get involved in."

"I'm sorry too." The Briton took his gun and headed for the door. "Thank you for your time, Clint."

"Sure," the Gunsmith replied. "Good luck— whatever you decide to do."

# FIVE

Talo, California didn't prove to have a very prosperous market for a traveling gunsmith. By the end of the day, Clint Adams hadn't found a single customer and Sheriff Sloan still seemed to be looking for a reason to either run Clint out of town or lock him up. The Gunsmith decided he'd be wise to move on in the morning.

Clint entered the local general store. Stacks of flour, grain and coffee were piled in a corner; kegs of pepper, nails and gunpowder formed columns along the walls; rifles and shotguns were mounted in racks behind a display case containing an assortment of revolvers and holsters. A familiar, lovely face gazed at the Gunsmith from behind the counter.

"Hello, Clint." Jenny Parker smiled. "Looks like I've surprised you again, huh?"

"You mentioned that your sister's husband owns the store," the Gunsmith said. "But you didn't tell me you worked here."

"Just filling in for Ted so he could spend a little time with Annie," she explained. "Since I showed up, they haven't had too much time together alone . . . until last night, of course."

"I'm sure they appreciate your consideration,"

Clint remarked. "I need to buy some possibles for the trail."

"Oh." Jenny's smile vanished. "You're leaving so soon?"

"Tomorrow morning," he replied.

"I didn't know you'd be going already." She shrugged. "But I guess that's the kind of man you are."

"I'm a drifter, Jenny," Clint told her. "I'm not the sort of man that stays in any one place for long."

He didn't need to add that he wasn't the type of man who'd settle down and raise a family either. Jenny had known that from the beginning. She smiled once more.

"See you tonight?" she asked.

"If you want." He nodded.

"I do. Now, what can I get you in the way of merchandise?"

"I need some coffee, a few tins of sardines, about four cans of tomatoes, a bag of flour and some beef jerky."

"Okay," Jenny said, jotting down the items on a notepad. "Anything else?"

"A couple boxes of forty-five-caliber lead slugs," the Gunsmith said. "Two hundred and forty grain, if you've got it."

"We have whole cartridges in stock."

"I prefer to load my own shells," Clint explained. "That way I can measure the powder myself and I'm sure how much goes into each cartridge."

"If that's what you want," the girl agreed, adding the item to her list.

"Okay if I pick up this stuff in the morning? Say, about eight o'clock?"

"Sure," Jenny agreed. "We'll hold it for you till

then. You can pay for everything when you pick it up."

"Thanks, Jenny," the Gunsmith told her. "Hey, do you want to have dinner tonight?"

"I can eat with anybody," she replied. "Let's not waste any time tonight."

*Lord, give me strength*, the Gunsmith thought, but he managed to smile and wink at Jenny.

# SIX

"How much?" a harsh masculine voice hissed from within the alley between the general store and the bank.

"There *isn't* any reward" a woman replied angrily.

Clint Adams emerged from the store in time to hear the strained conversation. He glanced around the corner and saw two men and a woman in the alley. A stocky, broad-shouldered character held the girl's arms from behind. His tall, lean partner pinched her jaw between the fingers and thumb of one hand as he stared intently at the captive.

The tall man wore a loose-fitting cattleman's slicker and a Montana peak hat with a shapeless brim. His heavy-set friend was clad in a corduroy jacket and a floppy ten-gallon hat. Clint could see little of either man's face, yet something seemed familiar about the pair.

The Gunsmith was certain he'd never seen the girl before. He would have remembered her if he had. She appeared to be in her late twenties, fair skinned with light brown hair and classically beautiful features. The girl's mouth was wide and sensuous, her forehead and cheekbones high. A pair of wire-rimmed glasses were perched on the bridge of her compact nose. The girl's gingham dress did not conceal the shapely curves of her figure from Clint's appreciative eye.

"What do you mean 'there ain't no reward'?" the man in the slicker growled. "Don't you lie to us, girl!"

"She's askin' to get hurt," the other man remarked with a high-pitched giggle that sounded as out of place from the stocky gruff ruffian as a buffalo chirping like a canary. "Ain't that right, Jake?"

"Reckon so, Mike," his partner replied.

*Jake and Mike*, Clint thought. *Jake Potter and Mike Crawley*. The Gunsmith remembered where he'd seen the two men before—in Waco about four years earlier. They'd hauled a corpse into town—a dead man who'd been shot in the back. The sheriff reluctantly paid them a two hundred dollar bounty for the corpse, which had formerly been a petty thief with a price on his head.

Potter and Crawley were the worst kind of professional bounty hunters. Unprincipled, ruthless and callous, they'd do anything for money. Potter and Crawley never brought a man in alive. Occasionally, they killed innocent victims, mistaken for wanted men. This never seemed to bother the regulators much.

They also had a reputation for beating information out of people. And it looked like the girl in the alley was about to be subjected to such a crude inquisition. Potter clamped his fingers on one of her large, ripe breasts.

"Now, let's try again," the bounty hunter began, cruelly twisting her nipple. "What about that reward?"

"I've got one for you right here, Potter," the Gunsmith announced as he stepped into the mouth of the alley and drew his modified Colt revolver.

The regulators turned to stare at Clint. Their eyes immediately fell to the .45 in his fist. Clint saw their faces clearly now. Potter's was gaunt with sunken, pitted cheeks and a hawk-bill nose dividing two close-set pig-eyes. Crawley's features were broad with a flat nose, thick lips and a droopy brow. The two looked like they were having a contest to see which man could be uglier.

"Let her go," Clint ordered, thumbing back the hammer of his pistol to add menace to his words. "Unless you want me to pay you off in lead."

"This business don't concern you, Adams," Potter said, but he stepped away from the girl.

Crawley released her. "We don't poke 'round in your doin's, Gunsmith," he whined.

"Unbuckle your gunbelts, boys," Clint instructed. "Ma'am, you move away from those two, but be careful not to step between either of them and my gun."

The bounty hunters dropped their gunbelts and the girl slowly moved away from the pair. Potter suddenly shoved her forcibly, sending the young woman stumbling into the Gunsmith. Clint managed to catch her, swooping his left arm around her waist. He swung the pistol toward the bounty hunters, but Potter and Crawley had already charged forward.

The regulators pounced. Potter grabbed for Clint's wrist behind the revolver, but Clint jerked his arm away from the bounty hunter's groping fingers and swiftly backhanded the gun barrel across the side of Potter's head. The bounty hunter crumbled to the ground.

Crawley's attempt to disarm Clint was more successful. The stocky regulator grabbed Clint's wrist with one hand and balled the other into a fist to punch Clint in the stomach. The Gunsmith groaned as the blow drove the wind from his lungs. Crawley was a strong son of a bitch. He seized Clint's wrist with both hands and twisted hard. The pistol fell from the Gunsmith's grasp.

Clint swung his left arm high and chopped the bottom of his fist into the nape of Crawley's neck. The bounty hunter grunted. Clint hammered Crawley's neck again and slammed a knee into his opponent's paunchy gut.

The Gunsmith wrenched his right arm from Crawley's grasp and drove a solid uppercut to the bounty hunter's jaw. Crawley's head bounced upward from the punch and Clint hit him in the face with a left hook. The combination punches staggered the regulator. Clint swung a right cross at Crawley's head, hoping to finish off his opponent, putting all his weight behind the punch.

Clint missed.

The momentum of his swing threw the Gunsmith off balance. Crawley took the opportunity to move behind Clint and slip his arms under the Gunsmith's armpits; he clamped his hands together at the back of Clint's head.

"I'm gonna bust yore neck!" the bounty hunter snarled, applying force to the full nelson hold.

Clint pressed his palms into his own forehead to ease the pressure of the wrestler's grip. He glanced at the wall of the general store less than a yard away. Without hesitation, Clint thrust both feet from the ground, knees touching his chest. Then he shot out his legs and drove the soles of his boots into the wall.

The kick shoved the Gunsmith and Crawley backward. The bounty hunter staggered into the bank, his back connecting hard with the brick wall. Clint snapped his arms down sharply and broke Crawley's hold on his neck.

The Gunsmith's head jerked back hard, butting his skull into Crawley's face. Then he rammed the point of an elbow into the regulator's ribs. Crawley moaned and began to sag against Clint's back.

Whirling, the Gunsmith slashed the back of his fist across Crawley's face. The bounty hunter's mouth and nose dripped blood as his knees buckled. Clint wasn't finished with his opponent. He drove an uppercut to the man's solar plexus and hit him in the temple with a left hook. Crawley slumped against the bank wall and sank to the ground in a senseless heap.

The triple click of a single-action revolver hammer being cocked startled the Gunsmith. *I didn't hit Potter hard enough*, he thought, raising his hands as he began to turn.

The girl held a revolver in her hands, the barrel pointed at Jake Potter. The regulator was on his knees, arms extended overhead in surrender. Clint's .45 lay on the ground two feet from Potter.

"He tried to grab your gun," the girl explained. For the first time, Clint noticed she spoke with a British accent.

"Thanks," he said.

The Gunsmith suddenly stepped forward and lashed out a boot, kicking Potter in the center of the chest. The bounty hunter fell to the ground and Clint quickly scooped up his pistol.

"That was for roughing up the lady, Potter," Clint explained.

"What the hell are you up to now, Adams?" Sheriff Sloan demanded as he jogged into the alley with a long-barreled Virginia Colt Dragoon in his fist.

"Teaching a couple of rude fellas some manners, Sheriff," the Gunsmith replied.

"I've had all the smart talk and trouble I'm gonna take from you, mister!" the lawman snapped. He aimed his pistol at Clint's chest. "Drop your gun. I'm taking you to jail!"

"What on earth for?" the girl asked. "This gentleman came to my rescue after these two men assaulted me. I shudder to think of what would have happened if he hadn't arrived when he did."

"You sure about that lady?" Sloan frowned, taking her in. "Yeah, course you are." The lawman kicked Crawley in the ribs. "Get up!" he snapped. "We don't hold with no goddamn rapists in this town, boy!"

"We can explain what happened, Sheriff," Potter said, breathing hard and massaging his head with one hand and his breastbone with the other.

"You'll do your talking in a jail cell," Sloan replied. "Looks like your friend is out cold, so you'll have to drag him over to the jailhouse."

"Hold on a minute," Potter began.

"I ain't in a good mood, feller," Sloan warned. "I disremember ever feeling more spiteful than I do right now, so you keep rubbin' me the wrong way and you'll wind up in Boot Hill insteada my jail. You savvy, boy?"

"All right, Sheriff," Potter agreed glumly. He glared at Clint and added. "I'll settle with you later, Adams."

The Gunsmith shrugged.

# SEVEN

Jake Potter grabbed Mike Crawley by the ankles and dragged his unconscious partner to the jailhouse. Sheriff Sloan escorted the bounty hunters, cursing and threatening them every step of the way. Clint turned to the girl and politely touched the brim of his stetson.

"You okay, ma'am?" he inquired.

"Yes," she replied, straightening the glasses on her nose. The eyes behind the lenses were light hazel with flecks of green. "Thanks to you—Adams, correct?"

"I'd rather you call me Clint," he grinned.

"That's a nice, rugged sort of name," the girl remarked. "Very American."

"Is your name very British?" he asked.

"I'm Janice Powers," she answered. "Does it sound terribly British to you?"

"Not as British as Edward Wardell," he replied.

"Oh?" she raised her eyebrows. "I take it you've already met Dr. Wardell?"

"That's right," Clint confirmed. "I figured you must be connected with him somehow. Lincoln is too small and isolated to attract two Britons for totally different reasons."

"I'm assisting Dr. Wardell," she explained. "I'm a zoologist—at least I will be when I've earned my degree. My expertise is primates. That's why I'm here.''

"To hunt for the sasquatch?'' Clint shook his head in disbelief.

"Correct,'' Janice answered. "The creature appears to be a totally different species of primate, so far unclassified in zoology. We don't know if it's an advanced breed of ape or a race of men that hasn't evolved to the level of true human.''

"Or it's just an Indian ghost story,'' Clint added.

"Then you regard the sasquatch as a mere legend and not an actual living creature?''

"I already had this conversation with Wardell, Janice,'' the Gunsmith replied. "I've got my own theories about Bigfoot and they don't include Charles Darwin.''

"You're familiar with Darwin's *The Origin of the Species*?'' the girl inquired.

"Can't say that I've read it,'' Clint confessed. "But I've heard about Darwin's theory that man descended from the apes. . . . ''

"That's not what Darwin claims,'' Janice explained. "He says that all life has evolved to best suit its environment. For example, fish evolved into amphibians when certain species left the water to live on land. Darwin presents proof of this with records of fossils of prehistoric life forms and we can actually see this change occurring in the lungfish which actually walks out of water onto the shore for short periods of time.

"Of course, the process of evolution requires thousands if not millions of years to develop a new species. Darwin's theory states that men and the apes may have had a common ancestor, but they obviously developed into very different species.''

''That notion is still contrary to the Bible,'' Clint remarked. ''Folks in this country don't care much for atheist theories.''

''Charles Darwin is not an atheist,'' the girl insisted. ''He acknowledges the existence of a Creator in *The Origin of the Species*. One might call Darwin a deist, a person who believes in God but doesn't embrace any established religion.''

''To most folks' way of thinking, that makes him an atheist.''

''Indeed?'' Janice raised her eyebrows. ''Then a good many of the Founding Fathers of the United States were atheists as well. Thomas Jefferson, for one, was a deist. Benjamin Franklin was an agnostic and tended to be quite vocal about his beliefs. Your Bill of Rights grants and guarantees freedom of religion for all faiths.''

''But there still isn't any proof that Bigfoot is anything but a legend based on exaggerated tales about mountain men and peyote pipe dreams.''

''People claimed the gorilla was just a myth until it was 'discovered' in 1858.''

''Gorillas are found in Africa, not California,'' the Gunsmith stated. ''I'm not an expert on monkeys and apes, but it seems to me they're always native to jungle regions, which wouldn't include the American Northwest.''

''That's not true at all,'' Janice replied. ''The langur monkey and the hoolock gibbon are native to the snowy mountains of the Himalaya where the *yeti* has been reported. There are also snow monkeys found in northern Japan. And how do you explain the Gibraltar apes? They're not supposed to be in Europe either, you know.''

''Apes were featured in circuses in Europe and I suppose the animals wound up in Gibraltar that way.'' Clint shrugged. ''I'd really rather not stand around in this alley and argue with a beautiful woman about monkeys, apes and Bigfoot.''

The girl grinned. ''It does seem a bit absurd to quarrel so with a knight in shining armor like yourself. After all, you not only rescued me from those two, you've also paid me my first genuine compliment I've received since I arrived in this country.''

''You've obviously been associating with the wrong sort of men, Janice,'' the Gunsmith told her.

''Perhaps.'' She shrugged. ''I suppose the glasses put them off a bit.''

''If any man fails to recognize your beauty,'' Clint said, ''*he* ought to be wearing glasses himself.''

''Such flattery.'' Janice laughed, delighted with Clint's charm. ''It's a pity Dr. Wardell and I will be leaving tomorrow. I'd rather like to stay awhile and get to know you better.''

''I'm moving on in the morning myself,'' Clint informed her.

''Really?'' Janice inquired. ''Doctor Wardell and I are looking for a guide—an experienced woodsman and tracker who knows the California forests. Ideally, someone who is also good with a gun. Would you be interested in the job? You don't have to believe in the sasquatch to help us hunt the creature.''

''Wardell already made that offer,'' Clint answered. ''But it sounds a lot better coming from you.''

''Then you accept?'' she asked eagerly.

"Sorry." He sighed. "I'm okay with a gun, but I'm hardly an expert tracker and I don't know the area well enough to act as a guide. Besides, I've got other plans."

"That's too bad." Janice frowned.

"Why were Potter and Crawley bothering you?" Clint asked. "I've never heard of those two being interested in anyone or anything unless they smelled a bounty."

"Oh." She rolled her eyes in frustration. "Those fools must have overheard Dr. Wardell refer to the sasquatch as the greatest potential discovery in the history of archaeology or zoology. They're convinced there must be a large reward offered for the beast. They were grilling me for information when you arrived."

"I can't imagine a bounty poster for Bigfoot." Clint chuckled. "It would look like an advertisement for a sideshow."

Janice scowled at the remark. "Well, there isn't any reward offered for it. The discovery would be of value only as a contribution to science."

"If you say so." Clint shrugged. "I'm not going to argue with you anymore."

"Good," Janice replied. Then she stepped forward and placed her lips against Clint's. The kiss was quick, but long enough for the Gunsmith to appreciate the taste of her soft, wide lips.

"Thanks again, Clint," Janice said.

With that, she hurried away.

# EIGHT

A projectile whistled past the Gunsmith's left ear. Clint jerked his head aside in a reflex reaction and pulled his Colt from leather. Porcelain shattered when the thrown object hit the wall behind him.

Clint had just opened the door to his hotel room and someone had hurled a water pitcher at him. He immediately holstered his revolver when he recognized his assailant.

"Jesus," he rasped. "What the hell's wrong with you, Jenny?"

"You son of a bitch!" Jenny Parker snarled as she picked up the washbasin from the dresser in Clint's room.

"Jenny—" he began.

She threw the bowl, her arm executing a sideways swing which sent the basin rocketing at him like a meteor. Clint barely ducked beneath the spinning projectile in time. It sailed into the hallway and crash-landed on the floor.

"You're supposed to spend one lousy night with me," Jenny began, grabbing Clint's saddlebags from the end of the bed. "But you're still trying to get that Limey bitch to go to bed with you, you randy bastard!"

She swung the saddlebags in a manner similar to a Greek hammer throw. Clint raised his arms and managed to catch the bags as he kicked the door shut. *Shit,* he thought. *Jenny's turning everything in the room into a goddamn weapon! It's a wonder she didn't kill her husband before the Apache got him. Maybe she did!*

Clint tossed the saddlebags aside as Jenny reached for the coal-oil lamp on a table. He dashed forward and scooped an arm around the girl's trim waist. She pounded her fists against his shoulders and back as he picked her up and kept moving to the bed.

Jenny rammed a knee into the Gunsmith's stomach before they hit the mattress. He cursed under his breath as he tried to pin her down. Jenny was a lot stronger than she looked and she struggled like a cornered bobcat. She even managed to punch him on the side of the jaw hard enough to spin Clint's head around.

Luckily for Jenny, Clint's code of chivalry and his temper held fast and he didn't hit her back. He caught Jenny's wrists and straddled her belly to pin her to the mattress. The girl's legs thrashed wildly, hammering her knees into the small of his back.

"Damn it!" he snapped. "Will you calm down and let me explain things to you?"

"I saw you kissing that English floozy!" Jenny hissed, still struggling in Clint's grasp.

"*She* kissed *me,*" he insisted. "Just one little kiss to thank me for saving her from those two bounty hunters the sheriff hauled over to the jailhouse today. Or didn't you see *that*?"

"You telling me the truth?" she asked suspiciously.

"Hell, Jenny," Clint groaned. "I came back to my room alone, didn't I? I plan to spend the night with you—unless you want to fight and argue instead of make love."

"Oh," she said, finally lying still beneath him. "I

guess I sort of jumped to conclusions.''

"Yeah,'' the Gunsmith muttered as he climbed off the bed.

Clint headed for the door. He glanced into the hallway to discover the doors of two other rooms were open and the heads of tenants stuck out of them to stare back at Clint.

"Good evening, folks,'' he said with a weak smile.

"What's goin' on up here?'' the desk clerk piped in a reedy voice as he cautiously mounted the stairs, holding a broom for a weapon.

"No problem, friend,'' Clint assured him, hurrying to the head of the stairs. "I just knocked over the washbasin and pitcher in my room.''

"How'd you manage that?'' the desk clerk asked.

"Just clumsy, I guess,'' Clint replied, hoping none of the tenants would mention that the shattered remnants of the objects in question lay scattered across the floor of the hallway.

"Well, I ain't gonna clean it up for you, mister,'' the man declared.

"I wouldn't ask you to,'' the Gunsmith replied. "I'll be glad to see to that myself, if you'll let me borrow that broom.''

"All right,'' the desk clerk agreed. "But we ain't got no extra pitcher or washbasin for you to replace 'em with and we'll have to charge you for the ones you busted.''

"Okay.'' Clint nodded. "Can I have that broom now?''

The desk clerk surrendered the broom and descended the stairs. One of the other tenants uttered a half chuckle, half snicker before retreating into his room. The Gunsmith swept up the broken porcelain and returned to his room, slightly red-faced with anger and embarrassment.

However, when Clint Adams found Jenny seated on the edge of the bed, his mood improved. She was naked and smiled sheepishly at him as he entered the room and shut the door.

"I see you've made yourself comfortable," Clint remarked. He was still irritated by the incident, but his male hormones were urging his emotions in a different direction.

"I sort of hoped you might not stay angry with me so long this way," she replied, explaining her nudity.

"Uh-huh," he muttered, not quite ready to forgive her.

"I'm really sorry, Clint," Jenny assured him.

"Okay," Clint said, joining her on the bed. "Let's forget it."

"I didn't hurt you, did I?" she asked, gently touching his face.

"You sure as hell tried hard enough," he complained.

"Thought you wanted to forget it" Jenny said. "Well, maybe I can make up for what I've done."

She leaned closer and pressed her lips against his cheek. Clint turned and kissed her mouth firmly. His right arm snaked around Jenny to pull her closer while his left hand fondled her breasts and gently teased the nipples. Their tongues slid into each others' mouths and Clint's hand trailed along her bare flesh to caress her naked thighs.

She fumbled with his shirt buttons and Clint decided it was time to undress. He stripped quickly. Jenny smiled with appreciation as she watched. When the Gunsmith returned to the bed, the girl was lying on her back.

He joined Jenny on the mattress, skillful fingers stroking her skin. She moaned with pleasure as Clint lowered his mouth to her breasts. He kissed and sucked gently while his hands roamed across her body. The Gunsmith's touch found her thighs and began to tenderly rub the golden triangle between them.

His lips moved down to her belly, tracing his tongue around the rim of her navel. Jenny gasped as he inserted a finger into her womanhood. Slowly, Clint shifted his face to her love chamber. He probed the lips of her vagina with his tongue and gradually worked it deeper.

"Oh, Clint!" Jenny cried. "Don't make me wait any longer! I'm ready! Sweet Jesus, I'm ready!"

The Gunsmith mounted her. Jenny's fingers found his manhood and fondled it with her usual magic touch. She didn't spend much time stroking him because his member was already swollen and erect. Jenny steered his throbbing cock into her love center.

Clint rotated his hips to gradually drive his penis deeper. Jenny pumped her loins, drawing him in. The Gunsmith responded to her urgency and increased the tempo of his thrusts. She bucked and quivered under him, rapidly approaching a climax.

The Gunsmith realized this and rammed himself home. She cried out as he continued to plunge his stiff member again and again. Then she cried out and trembled in a wild orgasm. Clint held her, kissing her neck and breasts, before he drove his hard cock inside her womanhood again.

The girl gasped and whimpered in ecstasy, wrapping

her arms around his neck. Jenny's long, strong legs encircled his hips as another orgasm overwhelmed her. She gyrated and bounced while Clint finally disgorged the hot, creamy load from his aching manhood.

"Oh, God," Jenny said, locked in a lover's embrace. "I'm so glad we had this night together, Clint."

"The night isn't over yet," the Gunsmith whispered.

# NINE

"I really should have gotten some sleep while I was in bed last night," Clint Adams said as he led Duke from his stall.

The horse breathed hard through his teeth, his vibrating lips making a sound of disgust.

"Okay," the Gunsmith growled, "don't be so critical. You ready to leave this town?"

Duke neighed with enthusiasm and bobbed his head while he pawed the ground with a forehoof. Perhaps the horse merely responded to the tone of Clint's voice, but no one would ever convince the Gunsmith Duke didn't understand him.

"Yeah," Clint said. "Me too."

He led Duke to the wagon, which was already hitched to the team and waiting outside the livery stable. Clint hitched his prize Arabian gelding to the back of the rig and climbed into the driver's seat.

The Gunsmith rode his wagon the hundred or so yards to the general store to pick up his supplies. Jenny Parker met him at the door.

"Figured I'd say good-bye," she explained. "Thanks for everything, Clint. I'll think about you a lot."

"Remember the good times, Jenny," he replied.

"But don't dwell on the past. Memories can be poison if that's all you have in your life."

"The voice of experience?" Jenny smiled.

"You might call it that." Clint grinned. "Or you might just say it's some friendly advice from somebody who cares."

"You take care of yourself, Clint Adams," she said gently. "You're a good man, but you sure have a way of getting yourself into trouble."

"I'll be careful," he assured her. "You do likewise, promise?"

She kissed him tenderly on the mouth and retreated into the store. Clint loaded his goods onto the wagon and rode out of Talo, California with no intention of ever returning.

The Gunsmith didn't know how quickly he'd have reason to change his mind.

The Northern California forests are spectacular. One of the largest woodlands in the world, it is filled with lush green grass, a variety of evergreen trees—including the magnificent Sitka spruce which can grow over two hundred feet high—and countless other types of trees, ferns, bushes and other plants.

The terrain became surprisingly difficult as the Gunsmith rode his wagon deeper into the forest. The trees and bushes grew very close together, forming solid walls of vegetation. Dense carpets of giant ferns, tall grass and weeds concealed dozens of fallen branches, some too large and heavy to allow Clint to move or ride over.

"Damn it," he muttered. "Where the hell is the road?"

He consulted his map, a copy of a government

surveyors' chart. It didn't help much. Made in 1859, it told of wagon paths and foot trails which had become covered by vegetation over the years. All Clint could be sure of was that he was somewhere between the Trinity Mountains and Willow Creek.

"I'm going to have to hack through this shit," Clint declared as he climbed down from the wagon.

He walked to the rear of the rig to get a corn knife from his gear. "Let's hope we can find something that resembles a road around here, big fella," he said to Duke.

The big Arabian wasn't listening. Duke pawed the earth and backed away from the wagon, about to pull the guidelines taut. He was strong enough to break the rope and seemed about to do exactly that. The animal raised his head and whinnied with alarm.

"What is it, Duke?" Clint asked, his hand falling to the Colt on his hip. "What's wrong?"

He'd been with Duke since the horse was a colt and he'd learned to respect Duke's ability to sense danger. The gelding had a nose like a bloodhound and ears that could pick up sounds a mile away. Duke was trying to warn Clint, but the Gunsmith had never seen his horse behave in such a desperate, frightened manner before.

Then Clint smelled something—a thick, musky scent, as if the bodies of a dozen skinned beavers had been left in the sun to rot. The other horses sensed it too and they neighed in terror, shuffling their hooves backward, moving the rig in the process.

"Whoa!" Clint shouted at the team as he hurried from the rear of the wagon.

Then he saw it.

A huge figure was crouched by a clump of bushes. It

was covered with dense dark brown hair, yet Clint saw muscles move beneath the hirsute coat as the thing extended a long thick arm into the bushes to uproot one as easily as a man might pluck a flower. It pulled the plant to its mouth. Clint heard the creature bite and chew its prize.

"My God," he whispered, dumbfounded. "It can't be . . ."

The beast had its back turned to the Gunsmith, but it seemed to stiffen at the sound of Clint's voice. It slowly rose to full height. Clint's mouth fell open as he realized the beast was more than seven feet tall.

Its shoulders were enormous, the skull tall and pointed with small ears. Clint saw that the hair extended from the creature's skin. It wasn't wearing a fur coat or cap. It sure as hell wasn't a bear with a head shaped like that. And Clint had seen the thing's hand clearly! It had four fingers and a thumb.

The beast turned its head slightly. Clint glimpsed a sloped forehead and a prominent cheekbone jutting from the creature's face. Suddenly, the thing bolted into the thick brush as though the forest were comprised of shredded newspaper.

Clint watched the big brown shape cut through the vegetation. *Nothing that big can move that fast*, Clint thought. Of course, bison and grizzlies are large animals capable of surprising speed . . . *But this thing runs on its hind legs like a man!*

Within seconds, the creature had disappeared into the forest.

The horses finally relaxed. They were still uneasy, but Clint knew they were no longer on the verge of panic. The Gunsmith patted Duke's neck.

"Don't worry, big fella," he told the Arabian. "We're getting out of here. In fact, we're going to turn around and head—"

A strange wail seemed to fill the forest. The Gunsmith had never heard anything like it before. His flesh crawled and his stomach knotted. The cry sounded like a coyote's howl blended with the haunting call of a distressed puma. Yet, there was a disturbing human quality to the wail.

"Like I said before," he remarked, "let's get the hell out of here."

# TEN

"Is that job still available?" Clint Adams asked.

The Gunsmith had returned to Talo and searched the town for Dr. Edward Wardell and Janice Powers. He found them together in the diner, eating lunch. The scientists were surprised by his unexpected appearance and his sudden interest in their expedition.

"Well, we finally found a guide," Wardell answered. "But he's not much with a gun."

"I'd like to come along as your troubleshooter," Clint stated.

"The job doesn't pay much, you know," Wardell warned. "I can only offer you thirty-five dollars. . . ."

"I'm not interested in the money," the Gunsmith replied. "I just want to be part of the expedition."

"What changed your mind, Clint?" Janice inquired.

"Remember I said I'd believe in Bigfoot when I saw one?" he began. "Well, I believe in it now."

The Britons stared at Clint as if he'd just sprouted wings and a halo and promised to tell them what Heaven was like.

"You actually encountered a sasquatch?" Wardell asked.

"Yeah," Clint nodded. "About six miles north of here."

"Well, sit down and tell us about it," the Briton urged.

The Gunsmith recalled the incident in detail. Wardell and Janice listened intently to every word, their expressions revealing unfettered excitement.

"Clint," Wardell began, "would you say it seemed more like an ape or a human being?"

"I don't know," the Gunsmith answered. "It sure as hell didn't look human—at least, not like any human I've ever heard of. I can't honestly say I've seen enough apes to be sure if that's what Bigfoot is or not."

"You mentioned a pointed head," Janice remarked. "The lowland African gorilla has a skull that shape. They have been known to be over six and a half feet tall."

"Yes," Wardell agreed. "But don't forget, Fuhlrott discovered the bones of a prehistoric man near Düsseldorf about ten years ago. The bones are believed to be almost eighty thousand years old."

"That's the one they're calling the Neanderthal man." Janice nodded.

"Correct," Wardell said. "A skeleton of Neanderthal was reconstructed and its skull indicates a pointed head as well.

"I know," the girl agreed. "But the skeleton belonged to a humanoid less than four feet tall. That's considerably smaller than the creature Clint saw today."

"The Neanderthal skeleton tells us the size of *one* prehistoric man," Wardell replied. "We can't be certain it represents the average height of the species. If Neanderthal, or a similar species, has survived with limited evolutionary changes, there's no reason to believe it can't be as varied in height as *Homo sapiens*."

"That sounds like Latin for queer," Clint muttered, aware he was being ignored by the scientists.

"It's Greek and refers to modern man," Janice explained. "Look, Doctor, the average height for a man today is five and a half feet tall. Clint, for example, is about seven inches taller than normal. Why would a Neanderthal race evolve into giants?"

"You've been to the British colonies in Rhodesia." Wardell shrugged. "Why are the Zulu a race of giants? Some of them are over seven feet tall."

"And Henry Stanley recently reported Pygmy tribes in the Congo comprised of midgets," Janice answered. "Both cases are restricted phenomena, probably due to inbreeding which caused inherited traits in bone structure. That doesn't explain why the sasquatch, *yeti* and the other creatures like them found throughout the world are reported as giants. The size *must be* common to the species."

"Clint"—Wardell turned to the Gunsmith—"you said this creature moved like a man, on its hind legs. It walked, correct?"

"It *ran*. That thing sprinted out of sight as fast as a rabbit."

"You're the expert on primates, Janice," Wardell declared. "Apes run on all fours, right? Man is the only primate that runs on two legs. The sasquatch must be a primitive species of man."

"Or a primate of an advanced order we're not familiar with. . . ."

"I thought you two wanted to capture Bigfoot," Clint stated, "not sit around here and talk about it all day."

Wardell blinked. "Quite so. We should be on our way to investigate the area where Clint saw the sasquatch. Do you think you can find the locale again?"

"I'm sure of it, Doctor," the Gunsmith answered. "What about your guide? Who is he and how well does he know the area?"

"He was born and raised in the region," the Englishman replied. "He's a Huppa Indian named Koduc. His tribe is located near Willow Creek. He's an experienced woodsman and tracker, of course, and he's hunted game as far north as the Siskiyou Mountains and as far east as the Cascades."

"Uh-huh," Clint grunted. "And what's this mighty hunter doing in Talo?"

"Koduc lives in a small shed behind the saloon," Wardell admitted. "The owner lets him stay there and he sweeps up the tavern after it closes for the night."

"In other words, he's a broken down old drunk who lives to keep himself supplied with whiskey," the Gunsmith said dryly. "Sounds like a terrific guide."

"Koduc knows the region," Wardell insisted. "And his people are familiar with the sasquatch— although they refer to it as an *O-Mah*. Frankly, I don't think Koduc is too eager to go hunting for the creature. The Huppa seem to regard the *O-Mah* as something of a forest devil."

"I hope their opinion doesn't prove to be accurate," the Gunsmith said. "Whatever that thing is, it's big, fast and powerful. We've got to regard it as potentially dangerous. Very dangerous."

"We're aware of that," Wardell assured him. "That's why we want you with us."

"However," Janice began, "you do realize we want the sasquatch alive, don't you?"

"Yeah." The Gunsmith nodded. "And I hope you folks have a real good plan in mind about how to go about that."

"We've brought the necessary equipment," Wardell stated. "Nets, ropes and a cage designed to hold a full-grown gorilla."

"You plan to catch that thing in a net?" Clint's doubts flavored his tone. "Look, we're not talking about a goddamn butterfly. . . ."

"These nets are strong enough to hold any large primate," Janice assured him. "Regardless of its size or strength."

"Of course"—Wardell sighed—"if that fails, you may have to shoot the creature, Clint. I'm giving you that Parker-Hale big game rifle. That ought to bring down the sasquatch, wouldn't you say?"

"A sixty caliber ought to bring down anything short of Old Ironsides," Clint agreed.

"Speaking of shooting," Janice began, "when you saw the sasquatch today, why didn't you shoot it?"

"I've never been one to take a life—human or animal—without good reason," the Gunsmith replied. "The Bigfoot didn't attack me and I damn sure didn't intend to eat it, so I guess I just didn't feel I had a right to kill the beast. Besides, I'm not sure if it's animal or human."

"We should have the answer to that in the next few days," Wardell declared.

"Maybe." Clint shrugged, but he wondered if they might be better off to leave the sasquatch alone, whatever sort of creature it might prove to be.

Animal, man—or devil.

# ELEVEN

"I have to quit getting myself into this kind of shit," Clint muttered as he led the way through the forest.

Doctor Wardell's wagon followed Clint. It was a modified buckboard with a large eight foot square cage, bolted to the back of the rig. Janice claimed the bars were made of solid steel and no living creature could possibly break out of it.

The Britons' "sasquatch-catching" gear consisted of ropes, nets and three long poles. Clint wasn't impressed by the equipment. It looked puny and ineffective. He doubted it would be enough to capture the monstrous beast he'd encountered earlier that day.

The wagon didn't have many other supplies. The Britons had brought two suitcases, two sleeping bags, some canned goods, water and two lanterns with a keg of coal oil.

The Gunsmith had left his wagon and team in the livery stable back in Talo. The dense forest would be formidable enough for one vehicle to travel through, let alone two. Besides, eight wagon wheels and six horses would cause too much noise. The sasquatch would have heard them a mile away.

Koduc, the Huppa guide, rode behind the Wardell wagon. The Indian was a sorry sight, seated on his scrawny mule with a tattered blanket for a saddle.

Koduc wore shabby, poorly patched clothing and an ill-treated old cavalry cap. He carried a knapsack hung over one shoulder and a single canteen on the other. The old man's nut brown skin was as wrinkled as his rumpled old jacket, and he didn't carry a gun.

Clint noticed Koduc's hands trembled constantly. The old man's lips quivered from time to time and he'd wipe them with his fingers. The Gunsmith recognized the traits of a chronic alcoholic. He'd seen them before. His best friend, Wild Bill Hickok, suffered from habitual drunkenness. Clint had begun to develop the same destructive traits himself when he'd plunged into blind grief after the death of Hickok and tried to drown his sorrow in liquor.

He knew the syndrome. First one drinks to ease the pain. Then the reason is "to forget." Finally drinking is all that matters in life.

The saloon becomes a house of worship for a new religion. The bar is the pulpit and the bartender a mute priest who delivers the substance of faith. The bottle is a god and the alcoholic its slave.

Clint had been fortunate. He'd crawled out of the bottle before it could claim his soul. Koduc obviously hadn't managed to do the same. The Gunsmith could sympathize with the Indian, but he knew he couldn't help him. No one could help the old man unless he decided to try to help himself. The main concern that Clint had was that Koduc stay sober and do his job. He could only hope the Indian hadn't told Wardell he was an experienced tracker just to earn enough money for a couple cases of whiskey.

"This is it," Clint announced when they reached the spot where he'd encountered the sasquatch.

Clint dismounted while Wardell and Janice climbed

down from the wagon. The Gunsmith reached for the saddle boot on Duke's back and drew the Parker-Hale rifle from its scabbard. He wasn't used to the gun, which was heavier and more awkward than his Springfield. Sixty caliber or not, he wondered if bringing along the British weapon instead of his familiar carbine had been such a good idea after all. *Little late now*, he thought sourly.

"Where was the sasquatch?" Wardell inquired.

"Over there," Clint pointed at the tangle of brush.

"Let's have a look," the Englishman began as he marched toward the bushes.

"No!" Koduc snapped, surprising the others. "You wait here. You might trample *O-Mah* tracks or break twigs and rub against leaves that have story for us to read. I look first. Alone."

"When it comes to reading sign"—Clint grinned, pleased with Koduc's professional attitude—"you're the boss."

The Indian nodded. He moved into the brush, carefully watching the ground before placing his feet down and cautiously avoiding contact with the leaves and branches. Koduc examined the bushes for several minutes before he knelt and studied the ground for a while. Then he returned to investigating the plants.

"It's taking him quite a while," Wardell commented impatiently.

"If he rushed it he'd be apt to make mistakes," Clint replied. "Give him time, Doctor."

"I'd just as soon you called me Edward, Clint," Wardell told him.

"Okay." The Gunsmith grinned. "I don't know much about these things, Edward, but a good tracker always looks over a trail two or three times to make sure he doesn't miss anything. Clues can be subtle and Koduc wants to make sure he's found everything before he makes any conclusions about what he sees."

Finally, Koduc motioned with his arm to summon the others. The Gunsmith and the two Britons joined their guide among the bushes. Koduc pointed at a large, deep track resembling an enormous human footprint.

"*O-Mah*," he declared.

"Good Lord," Wardell whispered, sinking to his knees beside the track.

"It is a male *O-Mah*," Koduc stated. "Females aren't that big. This *O-Mah* weighs maybe six times as much as I do."

"How can you tell?" Clint asked.

"I compare how deep my footprint is with *O-Mah* track." Koduc shrugged.

"Oh," the Gunsmith said, surprised by the simple logic involved in tracking.

"Koduc's right!" Janice exclaimed. She knelt by the footprints, measuring them with a folding yard stick. "The animal that made these tracks must weigh close to eight hundred pounds!"

"Look at that print!" Wardell added. "Definitely humanoid! Only the width of separation of the toes suggests it *isn't* human!"

"*O-Mah*'s feet turned on earth here," Koduc stated. "That means he stood here and reached out to bushes he pulled up from ground."

"That's more than five feet away!" Wardell exclaimed. "The creature has quite a reach."

"You bet it does," Clint confirmed.

"*O-Mah* was eating berries and leaves from the plants," Koduc explained. "My people know about

*O-Mah*. He eats plants mostly. Sometimes eats grass-hoppers, frogs, the white worms found under rotten tree bark.''

"It's omnivorous," Janice remarked.

"Will you speak English?" Clint asked with exasperation.

"Omnivorous means it eats both plant and animal life," Janice answered. "The same as the great apes."

"And man," Wardell reminded her.

"*O-Mah* doesn't eat much meat," Koduc insisted. "He is bigger than any man and stronger than a bear, yet he does not kill deer or other large game. *O-Mah* does not take much that my people, the Huppa, need. He wants to be left alone and never bothers man unless man bother him first."

"Sounds like a rather docile creature," Janice commented. "I imagine its behavior patterns are rather similar to a gorilla."

"A gorilla?" Clint asked, obvious alarm in his tone.

"Gorillas might look like dreadful brutes," Janice explained, "but they're really the most shy and gentle of apes. Orangutans and chimpanzees are both far more dangerous. They tend to be more carnivorous than gorillas. That is, they eat more meat. Carnivores are predators and thus very aggressive and generally more dangerous."

"Has the *O-Mah* ever been known to harm any of your people, Koduc?" Wardell asked.

"Not in my lifetime," the Indian replied. "But it is said the *O-Mah* was once angered by hunters who shot arrows into him. Its vengeance was terrible. Many died."

"What happened?" Wardell inquired.

"The gods told our medicine man that the *O-Mah* is

a spirit of the forest. It is sacred . . . or so the story goes.''

''Do you believe it?'' Clint wanted to know.

''I have not been a true Huppa for many years,'' Koduc stated. ''I do not believe in my people's gods or the legends of *O-Mah*. I would not be here if I did.''

''I see.'' Wardell nodded. ''What happened with this *O-Mah* in the story? Did your people kill it?''

''The *O-Mah* had its revenge and returned to the forest.'' Koduc shrugged. ''My people could not kill it. Neither could the whites. *O-Mah* is a spirit that can not die from arrows or bullets. Nothing can kill the *O-Mah*.''

# TWELVE

They followed the tracks deeper into the forest. It was necessary to hack through tangled weeds and dense brush in order to make room for the wagon. Clint was stunned by the formidable foliage. He'd once been forced to journey into a Louisiana swamp while carrying out a mission for the U.S. government. Even that environment hadn't been as difficult as the Northern California forest.

At least there wasn't any quicksand or alligators in the woods, but he hadn't had to worry about a seven foot hairy monster in the swamp.

By dusk, they decided to set up camp for the night. Janice prepared a supper of salt pork, beans, bread and peaches. Everyone was tired and hungry after the long hours of hard work involved in clearing the trail. They all had hearty appetites and eagerly cleaned their plates.

"We'd better keep the campfire going tonight," Clint advised as he poured some coffee into a blue tin cup.

"We came here to find the sasquatch," Wardell declared. "Not to frighten it away."

"Look," the Gunsmith began, "do you want to tangle with that thing in the dark? I've seen it and I sure as hell don't want to meet it again under those conditions.''

"I suppose the beast would be rather difficult to capture at night,'' the Briton admitted, fishing out a briar pipe and a pouch of tobacco from his suitcase.

"It's going to be pretty difficult to capture Bigfoot regardless of when and where we find it,'' Clint replied. "Speaking of which—just how do you plan to go about that little miracle when the time comes?''

"We'll catch it in the net, of course,'' Janice answered.

"That's what you said.'' Clint sighed. "But you've got to realize that thing is over seven feet tall. We've had to hack through this forest until our arms are about to come out of their sockets, but the Bigfoot can plow through this place as if it were an open pasture. Does that give you some idea how strong it must be? Are you so sure we can catch it in a net?''

"Clint,'' Janice said, "those nets are made of the same sort of rope used by mountain climbers. I've helped capture gorillas in Africa. How do you think that's done? We didn't sprinkle salt on the ape's arse! We used nets, just like the ones we have in that wagon.''

"Oh, that's not all we brought,'' Wardell added, again reaching into his suitcase to extract a dark bottle. "This is chloroform, a very potent anesthetic similar to ether.''

"You think you can get *O-Mah* drunk?'' Koduc laughed. "I've got a bottle of red-eye. Figure we should use it too?''

"Hardly,'' Wardell replied dryly. "Anyway, we'll soak a cloth with chloroform and attach it to a pole. Then we'll hold the cloth out and place it over the beast's nose and mouth. The sasquatch inhales the fumes and passes out. . . .''

"You hope," Clint muttered.

"If it doesn't work," the Englishman said, "you may have to use that Parker-Hale blunderbuss, Clint.''

"You said you did not want to kill the *O-Mah*!" Koduc said in an alarmed voice. "You told me you would not kill him!''

"We don't intend to, unless we've no other choice," Wardell answered. "After all, the sasquatch—or *O-Mah* as you call it—is a very large, powerful animal which must be regarded as potentially quite dangerous.''

"I thought you said it can't be killed, Koduc," Clint remarked.

"And I told you of the Huppa legend," the Indian replied. "What will happen if we offend the *O-Mah*?''

"You told us you don't believe in those stories," Janice said.

"I believe enough to be afraid," Koduc explained, extracting a bottle from his pack. "The *O-Mah* is real. Maybe the stories are too.''

Clint realized there was no point in arguing with the Indian, who still retained the superstitions of his tribe. The Gunsmith decided it was time to change the subject. "Before you start sipping on that red-eye, I think we'd better decide about how we want to split up guard duty tonight.''

"Guard duty?" Wardell raised his eyebrows. "That's a bit extreme, don't you think?''

"No, I don't," Clint replied. "Who wants to stand first watch?''

"I will do it," Koduc offered. "I'd rather get it over with.''

"Fine," Clint agreed. "Take a nice big swallow from that bottle and hand it over. I'll give it back to you after your shift is over."

Koduc frowned. "You don't trust me, Clint Adams?"

"Can I trust you with a bottle on guard duty?"

"No," Koduc admitted. He took a single long drink of red-eye and surrendered his bottle to the Gunsmith.

Clint Adams was accustomed to life on the trail and sleeping under the stars in his bedroll with saddlebags for a pillow. However, he'd acquired the habit of combat sleep which allowed his muscles and nerves to rest while his subconscious remained alert to danger. Clint heard or felt the approach of footsteps as he lay in his bedroll by the wagon. He awoke instantly and prepared to reach for his gun.

"Clint?" Koduc whispered.

"I'm awake," the Gunsmith replied. He gazed up at the Indian through sleep-fogged eyes. "Is it time for my watch already?"

"No," Koduc began in a low, tense voice. "There's something out there. It is moving through the trees toward the camp."

The cobwebs of slumber melted away and Clint rose to his feet, fully awake, the modified Colt already in his fist.

"Where is it?" he asked, scooping up the Parker-Hale rifle.

"There." The Indian pointed at a treeline to the west. "I heard it moving, but I didn't see anything. Whatever it is, it's big and it's headed this way."

"Wake the others."

Clint moved to the cover of the wagon and holstered

his .45 in order to hold the rifle with both hands. He stared at the forest and waited. At first he heard nothing. Maybe Koduc had another bottle in his pack and he'd taken a few nips on duty after all, or the old man's imagination may have gotten the better of him. The Indian was shit-scared of the *O-Mah*.

*That makes at least two of us,* Clint thought.

Then he heard it. Leaves and twigs rustled loudly. Branches creaked as something shoved them aside. Koduc was right. Whatever was out there, it wasn't little.

"Clint, can you—" Wardell's voice began.

"Quiet," the Gunsmith hissed, concentrating on the approaching intruder.

He strained his eyes, trying to see something— *anything*—amid the black shadows of the trees. A shape gradually took form. A big, dark shape that walked on two legs; it was covered with dense brown fur from head to toe. . . .

"Hello, the camp!" a gruff voice called out. "I mean ye no harm, so I'd be obliged if'n ye don't shoot me."

"We never shoot peaceable folks," Clint replied. "That wouldn't be a friendly attitude."

"Purely ain't," the voice chuckled. "Mind if'n I enter yore camp?"

"Come ahead," Clint invited, but he turned to Koduc and Wardell. "Watch the surrounding area," he whispered. "This could be a diversion."

The stranger stepped into the clearing. The faint glow of the dying campfire illuminated the midnight visitor. At first glance, he appeared to be a sasquatch after all.

Six and a half feet tall, the figure was broad-shouldered with a huge barrel chest and thick, long arms. Brown hair indeed covered his entire body—buffalo fur. The face beneath a coonskin hat was dark and craggy, decorated by a long, dense black beard.

"I go by the handle of Bison Haggard," the mountain man announced.

Clint Adams and the others introduced themselves. Haggard nodded solemnly.

"I smelled coffee," the mountain man explained. "Ain't got much to trade for a cup or two unless you fellers can use some chewin' tobacco."

"Oh, you're welcome to some coffee, sir," Wardell invited.

"Ain't lookin' for no charity," Haggard said gruffly.

"Since we're camped in your territory, we're sort of neighbors right now," Clint stated. "Neighbors don't offer each other coffee out of charity."

Bison Haggard smiled. "Much obliged."

He strode to the campfire. Although the mountain man seemed amiable enough, he still presented a formidable appearance. Clad in the hides of wild animals, from the crown of his raccoon headgear to the soles of his beaverskin boots, Haggard looked like a barbarian. He carried a .56-caliber Sharps muzzle-loader tucked under his arm and a large bowie knife in a belt sheath. He squatted by the fire and Koduc poured him a cup of coffee.

"Thank ye." Haggard nodded. "I been out in the woods, away from my digs for quite a spell now. Run outta coffee couple days back. Purely is good of ye to give me some."

"Do you live out here?" Janice asked. Her tone suggested she'd find an affirmative answer difficult to believe.

"Yes, ma'am." Haggard smiled, his eyes wandering over the Englishwoman's body. Although she wore a checkered shirt and Levi's, Janice's feminine curves were obvious.

"Ye is a right purty gal," he remarked. "Ain't seen me no white woman since I disremember when."

"How come you're called Bison?" Clint inquired, wanting to get Haggard's attention away from Janice before he could get any lustful notions . . . although it was probably too late to prevent that. "There aren't any buffalo around here, are there?"

"Hell, no," the mountain man answered. "I ain't seen no buffalo since I left the Arizona Territory. Got me my handle back there when I hunted bison. The buffalo is gonna all be gone before long way things is these days. What with so many white hunters gunnin' down whole herds at a time. Some Injuns is just as bad 'cause they'll stampede bison over cliffs. Gonna kill 'em all if'n they keep doin' that way. Mark my word on that."

"How'd you wind up here?" Wardell asked.

"Drifted for a spell." Haggard shrugged. His eyes fell to the Parker-Hale rifle in Clint's grasp. "Fine lookin' weapon ye got there. Can't recall ever seein' one quite like it afore."

"I like it," the Gunsmith replied simply.

"Have you ever encountered any unusual animal life in the forest?" Wardell inquired.

"Depends on what ye be callin' unusual, friend," the mountain man answered as he sipped his coffee.

"Some call it Bigfoot," Clint explained.

"Bigfoot?" Haggard raised his thick black eyebrows. "Ye mean the forest devil? *O-Mah*, the Huppa call 'im."

"That's the one," the Gunsmith confirmed.

"Can't say as I'm sure I seen 'im, exactly," Haggard stated. "But I've smelled the devil's brimstone breath and I heard 'im howl more than once. Sounds like the wailin' of a damned soul acallin' outta Hell."

"Do you know where we might find this beast?" Wardell asked.

"Ye folks want to find the forest devil?" Haggard shook his head. "Me and the Huppa, we know 'bout the *O-Mah*. Best leave 'im be."

The mountain man rose. "I be on my way now. Sorta reckon we's even. Ye give me coffee and I'm gonna give ye some advice. Ye can take it or leave it, as is yore taste."

Haggard marched toward the trees, then he turned and said, "Don't go lookin' for the devil. Ye might find 'im. Or he might find ye first."

The mountain man headed into the forest. Within seconds he had blended into the shadows.

# THIRTEEN

The Gunsmith and his party continued to follow the sasquatch footprints. Koduc proved to be a very skilled tracker. Reading sign was very difficult in the dense forest, but the old Indian managed to find clues even on hard, dry surfaces that left no trace of a footprint that the others could see.

"How do you do it?" an amazed Edward Wardell asked Koduc.

"I have studied the *O-Mah* track for many hours," the Indian replied. "I know it as one knows the face of his brother. I do not have to see all of the track to recognize it now."

After two days, the others began to doubt their guide. They wondered if he'd made a mistake and led them in the wrong direction. Then, Koduc called them forward when he discovered a new clue on the side of a spruce tree.

"*O-Mah*," he announced. "Three, maybe four hours ago."

Tufts of long dark hair were lodged in the cracks of the bark. Janice and Wardell eagerly examined it and confirmed that the hair was identical to samples found where they'd first began to track the beast.

A few hours later, their expectations fell once more

when Koduc located some fresh tracks in mud at the shore of a stream.

"*O-Mah* has gone into the water," the Indian stated. "Even I can not read his sign now."

"Would an ape enter water?" Clint asked Janice.

"Some would," she replied. "Besides, we don't know what this creature is. It doesn't seem to be any sort of ape I'm familiar with."

"Maybe it just developed differently," Clint commented.

"What's that, Clint?" Wardell asked.

"I was just thinking about what you said about the Bering Strait," the Gunsmith replied. "If the Indians did cross over from Asia, maybe some apes did likewise."

"And eventually the apes changed their behavior patterns and certain physical characteristics to adjust to their new environment," Janice added. "If Darwin's theories about the development of a species is correct, *it is possible*."

"Why would they walk upright?" Wardell wondered.

"If they developed in a tundra region in the Yukon," Janice replied, "it's possible that the species was forced to stand and walk on their hind legs in order to reach leaves and thin branches when the rest of the ground would be blanketed by snow. They'd have to undergo a drastic change in diet, since there isn't any bamboo available in this country."

"And the sasquatch that migrated to this forest would also have to walk upright in order to pass between close-set tree trunks," Wardell commented. "Perhaps after a few thousand years, a species of ape could evolve into the beast we're tracking."

"But I doubt that it would be a very successful species." Janice sighed. "Apes, unlike man, have great difficulty adjusting to a new environment. The sasquatch seems to be quite rare, which isn't surprising. The new breed of apes would probably have trouble reproducing and their life span would tend to be rather short due to the shock caused by such radical changes to their inherited body structure. In a hundred years or less, they'll probably be extinct."

"Then only the legend will continue," Clint mused. "Well, whatever the answer might be—"

The Gunsmith's words ended in mid-sentence when he saw the column of figures that stood on the opposite side of the stream. Short, wiry men dressed in deerskin clothing, the Indians were armed with bows, arrows and lances. They had emerged from the treeline to stare at the four strangers to the forest that was their homeland.

"Huppa?" Clint asked Koduc.

The Indian guide nodded in reply.

"What do they want?" Wardell whispered.

"They're letting us know they're around," Clint answered. "If they just wanted to look at us, they could do that without exposing themselves. If they wanted to communicate or trade with us, they'd gesture for us to approach or just cross the stream to talk to us. Am I reading your people right, Koduc?"

"Yes," the guide agreed. "They do not approve of us. They are expressing their feelings to us by their actions."

"Will they attack?" Janice asked fearfully.

"They haven't fired any arrows or thrown a lance our way," the Gunsmith said. "This is just a warning."

The Huppa braves turned and walked into the forest as silently as a group of shadows. "Reckon they figure they've delivered the message," Clint remarked.

"Do you think they suspect we're stalking the sasquatch?" Wardell inquired.

"Maybe," Koduc said. "My people would not approve of that. It would be very bad medicine if the *O-Mah* is angered again."

"Huppa have never been much for fighting, way I hear it," Clint commented.

"That is true," Koduc nodded. "But they are many and we are few."

"Yeah," the Gunsmith agreed. "And they're probably more frightened of the *O-Mah*'s magic than our guns. And, frightened men can be dangerous."

# FOURTEEN

The expedition was faced with a choice—to continue to stalk the sasquatch or to turn back. They reluctantly decided to continue. Koduc suggested they follow the stream; he hoped to find sign of their quarry further up the bank. However, dusk was approaching, so they set up camp for the night.

"We'll have to check both sides of the stream for tracks," Koduc remarked as he arranged a stone circle for the campfire. "*O-Mah* seems to be moving toward the Siskiyou Mountains. He seems to favor that area."

"Mountains?" Wardell raised his eyebrows. "That's interesting. I don't believe apes generally favor mountains, but prehistoric man did. Caves provided a natural shelter and the high elevation was an advantage for lookouts to watch for danger and it was easier to defend against invaders."

"Janice would probably tell us about some mountain-climbing gorilla or cave-dwelling monkey," Clint muttered. "Where'd she get to anyway?"

"I suppose she's looking for firewood or hunting about for local animal species to study," Wardell replied.

"She shouldn't wander off from camp alone," the Gunsmith said, gathering up his canteens. "I'm going

to fill these. I'll look for Janice while I'm at the stream.
If she comes back, tell her what I said. On second
thought, I'll tell her myself.''

Clint strolled through the brush to the bank of the
stream. Sure enough, he found Janice Powers there.

The girl stood in the stream. The level of the water
rose above her hips and her back was turned to the
Gunsmith. Janice was stark naked. She scooped up
water and slowly washed her shoulders and neck.

He admired the graceful curves of her lovely body as
he stood in the bushes and watched her bathe. Janice
turned slightly and rubbed water over her breasts. Clint
felt his manhood stir as he watched her run her hands
over the magnificent white mounds. The English girl
was really quite beautiful, her figure perfect, her ivory
skin flawless. Janice cupped her breasts in her palms
and examined them briefly, thoughtfully teasing an
erect nipple.

Then she lowered herself into the water until her
breasts were submerged. Clint saw her head revolve
and a long, shapely leg rose from the surface. She
washed the lovely limb, caressing the knee and thigh
slowly.

''Oh, boy,'' Clint whispered, feeling his passion
build. ''Better come back for water some other time.''

Reluctantly, he pulled his eyes away from the girl.
The Gunsmith headed back to the camp, wishing
his erection wasn't rubbing against the crotch of his
Levi's.

Then Janice screamed.

Clint spun about and charged back to the stream,
drawing his .45 Colt as he ran. Janice was still in the
water, standing with her arms hugging her naked

breasts and her face pale with terror. Three figures stood at the shore. Clint only saw their backs, but he recognized all three men.

The huge, muscular figure of Bison Haggard was unmistakable, still clad in buffalo robe and coonskin cap. His lean companion in the cattleman frock and a stocky character dressed in a wrinkled corduroy jacket were equally familiar to the Gunsmith. *Potter and Crawley!* Clint realized. *How the hell did they get here? Sloan must have let them out of jail already. Or did they manage to escape?*

Not that it mattered at that moment. The trio threatened Janice. That's all Clint cared about. They advanced into the stream. Haggard had left his Sharps on the shore. Crawley giggled and began to unbutton his shirt. Potter silently waded toward Janice, hands outstretched, fingers arched like claws.

"You fellas wait your turn!" Clint shouted as he stepped from the bushes, the .45 in his fist. "You all need a bath, but let the lady finish hers first."

The trio turned and stared at the Gunsmith. Haggard bellowed in rage and splashed out of the water to reach for his rifle. Clint's revolver snarled and a burst of dirt spat from the ground between the mountain man's hand and the Sharps. Haggard drew back quickly and raised his arms overhead.

Jake Potter also reached for the clouds, but his partner figured he had a chance to blast the Gunsmith. Crawley took it. His hand streaked to the grips of a .44 Remington in a crossdraw holster on his belt.

Clint's Colt roared again and a .45 caliber lead messenger split Mike Crawley's forehead. The back of the bounty hunter's skull exploded and brains and

blood spewed across the stream. The corpse fell grace-
lessly, splashing water on Janice and Potter.

"Bass-turd devil!" Haggard snarled as he suddenly
bolted into a dead run.

The Gunsmith swung his revolver toward the fleeing
figure. He hesitated, reluctant to shoot an unarmed
man in the back. Clint whirled to cover Potter. The
bounty hunter's arms were still held over his head.

"Drop your gunbelt, Potter," the Gunsmith ordered. "Let it fall in the water."

"You ain't gonna shoot me, Adams," Potter declared as he moved backward, hands still raised high.

"Don't bet on it, Potter," Clint warned.

The bounty hunter smiled nervously as he kept back-
ing away. Clint fired and water jumped near Potter's
right hip. The regulator cried out in fear and desperately shuffled to the left. He suddenly slipped and fell
full length into the stream.

Potter splashed through the water to the opposite
side of the stream and scrambled onto the shore. Clint
held his pistol with both hands and aimed at the bounty
man and staggered to the treeline.

"Shit!" the Gunsmith groaned with exasperation,
still unable to squeeze the trigger and kill a man in cold
blood.

"Thank God you came when you did!" Janice
gasped as she hurried from the water. "Heaven knows
what would have happened otherwise!"

"Don't worry about that now," Clint said, glancing
about the surrounding forest. "Where'd they come
from?"

"I'm not sure," she replied. "I just looked up and
there they were." Janice reached for her clothes, lying

in a bundle on the shore. "Those two awful men from Talo were with Bison Haggard."

"Yeah," Clint nodded. "I recognized all three of them."

"What do they want?"

"Let's talk about that later," he urged, scooping up the .56 caliber Sharps abandoned by Haggard.

"This is so embarrassing," the girl remarked, hastily pulling on her plaid shirt and Levi's. "I just wanted to take a bath."

"Lady"—the Gunsmith grinned—"you don't have anything to be ashamed of."

# FIFTEEN

Doctor Wardell and Koduc heard the shots and joined Clint and Janice by the shore of the stream. They stared at the corpse of Mike Crawley which bobbed in the water, a crimson cloud forming around his bullet-shattered skull.

"Good Lord," Wardell whispered. "As if we didn't have enough worries already!"

"Well"—Clint shrugged—"we don't have to worry about Crawley anymore."

"He was one of the bounty hunters who assaulted me back in Talo," Janice explained.

"I thought you said the sheriff arrested those two," Wardell said.

"Well, they didn't stay in jail for long," the Gunsmith said.

"What do they want with us?" Koduc asked. "Are they after the woman?"

"They sure wanted her at the time," Clint said. "But their main goal is probably the same as ours. Potter and Crawley must think there's a bounty offered for Bigfoot and they're still determined to collect it."

"And they managed to convince Haggard to join them," Janice added.

"Do you think he was working for them the night he visited our camp?" Wardell asked.

"Well, he told us that ghost story about how Bigfoot is supposed to be the devil," Clint answered. "But Haggard doesn't really believe that crap or he wouldn't be acting as a guide for the bounty hunters. He told us that story to try to scare us off. He either wanted to protect his privacy for his own reasons or he wanted to get rid of competition for the sasquatch. Doesn't really make much difference either way. Haggard and Potter are partners and that's all that matters."

"Do you think they'll be back?" Wardell inquired.

"I'd say the odds are better than fifty-fifty," the Gunsmith replied grimly. "We'd better expect more trouble from those two."

Clint offered the Sharps rifle to Koduc. "You know how to use this?" he asked.

The Indian nodded and took the gun.

"You'll only have one shot," Clint told him. "Haggard didn't leave any ammunition for us."

"That is one more than I had before," the Indian remarked philosophically.

"I probably should have shot the other two bastards," Clint muttered, staring at the corpse of Mike Crawley.

"You've got principles, Clint." Janice smiled. "You couldn't morally justify shooting two unarmed men."

"We might wish I had. Those fellas will probably come back."

"I rather suspect they'll think twice about that now that they've seen how well you shoot, Clint," Janice remarked with frank admiration.

"Indeed," Wardell agreed, gazing at Mike Crawley's bloodied face. "You shot that chap right between the eyes."

Clint shrugged, glancing at the floating corpse. "Reckon it was a clean kill."

The night sky displayed a plethora of stars as the Gunsmith stood guard at the perimeter of the campsite. Clint was well-equipped to deal with any threat that might occur. In addition to the Parker-Hale rifle and the modified double-action Colt on his hip, Clint had also removed his New Line belly gun from a saddlebag and wore it tucked in his belt under his shirt. A diminutive .22-caliber pistol, the New Line was an excellent hideout piece and had saved the Gunsmith's life more than once.

Clint figured the circumstances merited as much firepower as possible. With Potter and Haggard, the Huppa Indians and the sasquatch all lurking somewhere in the surrounding forest, Clint wouldn't have felt secure if they'd had a dozen armed sentries on duty.

Darkness is a friend of the aggressor, not the defender. A man with good night vision could hide in the woods with a rifle or a sturdy bow and pick them off one by one. Clint was more concerned about Potter and the mountain man than the Huppa. It was unlikely the Indians would make such a drastic move after dark— not when the *O-Mah*, which they considered a supernatural being, stalked the area.

The bounty hunter and Haggard were far more apt to attack the camp at night. Bushwhacking and drygulching were Jake Potter's specialties. Bison Haggard probably knew the forests of California better than any white man. Together they were a formidable and treacherous team which had to be considered the greatest threat to the Gunsmith and his party.

Unless the sasquatch itself decided to take the offensive.

The man-beast was a different type of opponent, an unknown factor because it was neither human nor truly animal. If it did attack, what tactics would its primitive mind employ? Would the creature simply charge and resort to its considerable brute strength or was it intelligent enough to devise strategy and use weapons in combat?

Clint Adams shivered and turned up his collar although he knew the cool breeze had nothing to do with the icy tremble that traveled along his spine.

"Clint?" a familiar feminine voice called softly.

He turned to face Janice Powers as she approached. Moonlight reflected on the lenses of her glasses and a wide smile appeared on her tempting lips.

"I didn't get a chance to properly thank you for rescuing me today," she explained. "And this is the second time you've saved me too."

"My pleasure," he assured her. "Taking sides with a beautiful lady is sort of natural for me."

"Natural activities are often the best," Janice declared as she slipped her arms around his neck.

Their mouths crushed together in fierce passion. Clint ran his tongue over her teeth and probed the walls and roof of her mouth. His hands slowly descended to caress the girl's breasts which strained the fabric of her shirt. The Gunsmith unbuttoned the garment and slid a hand inside to feel the soft rounded flesh. Janice moaned with pleasure and nibbled at Clint's neck as her hands found the bulge in his trousers between his legs.

They kissed and fondled, savoring the prolonged foreplay. Janice gradually unbuttoned the Gunsmith's trousers. His stiffened member protruded from the gap, the cool air brushing its sensitive skin. Janice slowly sank to her knees and opened her mouth.

Wide soft lips slipped over the hooded head of his penis. Clint trembled as her mouth climbed the length of his shaft. Her tongue rolled over his erection. Janice took his full length, her lips touching the root of his stiff organ. Slowly, she moved her mouth up and down his cock, holding it in a warm, damp grasp.

The Gunsmith began to reach his limit. Janice sensed this in the manner of a woman experienced in the art of making love. She released his throbbing cock and began to undress.

The moon cast a pale spotlight on her alabaster skin as she dropped her shirt to the ground. Clint followed her example and disrobed, his fingers groping for buttons and buckles as his eyes remained fastened on the beautiful display of naked womanhood which unfolded before him.

The couple sank to the ground and continued to explore each other's bodies with fingers, mouths and tongues. The girl's legs parted and Clint straddled her, eagerly accepting the unspoken invitation.

His swollen manhood slid inside her. They gasped as the coupling began, embracing one another tightly. Clint's hips rotated to slowly work himself deeper. Janice began to pump herself to and fro, drawing him in.

"Clint!" she whispered breathlessly. "Yes, Clint!"

The Gunsmith skillfully increased the tempo of his thrusts. Janice moaned, trying to control her cry of delight as the first orgasm sent her into a glorious convulsion. Clint continued to drive himself into her, gasping in sensual pleasure.

Her fingernails streaked scarlet lines across his back as she approached a second climax. Clint's zenith had also arrived. He rammed himself faster, harder and carried them both beyond the brink. Together they found themselves in paradise and exploded in a mutual pinnacle of ecstasy.

# SIXTEEN

The following morning, Koduc found fresh tracks. The size of the manlike footprints left no doubt that they had once again picked up the trail of the sasquatch.

Clint Adams and his crew were filled with mixed emotions. The possibility of finding the elusive, legendary man-beast promised the excitement of a new discovery and the terror of confronting the unknown. They were also anxious about encountering the Huppa Indians or Potter and Haggard. The Gunsmith's party were the hunters, yet they were, most probably, the hunted as well.

They followed the inhuman footprints for hours. The tracks led them farther into the forest to a ravine. Koduc held up a hand to urge the others to stay put while he approached the rim of the gully alone.

He studied the ground with care and tread silently on moccasin-shod feet. The Indian was more cautious than ever as he drew toward the ravine. Koduc gazed into the valley. Then he turned and cat-footed his way back to Clint, Wardell and Janice.

"Do not raise your voice," he warned them in a tense whisper.

Wardell and Janice nodded in mute reply. Clint's fists tightened around the butt of his Parker-Hale rifle.

"The *O-Mah* is down there," Koduc explained.

"Are you certain?" Wardell rasped, his eyes wide with excitement.

"I am certain," the Indian confirmed. *"I saw it."*

They were all stunned by the statement. The Gunsmith was the first to recover. "Well, this is what we came for," he whispered.

Wardell nodded and led the way to the back of his wagon. The horses were still calm because the breeze hadn't carried the scent of the sasquatch to their nostrils. *If Bigfoot is really down there,* Clint thought.

"Dr. Wardell and I will handle the net," Janice said. "Clint, you and Koduc take the ropes."

No one argued with her authority. None of the others had previous experience at capturing African gorillas, so Janice had unquestionable credentials as the commander of this phase of the operation. Wardell attached rags to the ends of two poles and doused the cloth with chloroform.

They approached the ravine carefully, Koduc and Clint armed with a coil of rope and a rifle, Wardell and Janice each carrying a pole and the net extended between them. They reached the lip of the gully and gazed down.

Walls of earth and rock lined the ravine. Tall grass and ferns surrounded a pond in the center. A large, dark shape was crouched by the water. Its arms reached out to seize and uproot plants which it raised to its mouth.

*My God,* Clint thought. *We really found it!*

Stealthily, they crept over the ledge and down the walls of the ravine. The face of the gully was not steep and descending was simple enough. Sneaking up on the sasquatch was their real problem. The beast's sense of hearing and smell were no doubt far more acute than human. It might well detect them before the band could get close enough to attempt a capture.

The Bigfoot continued to feed on ferns and grass-roots as they closed in. Its size was awesome. The Gunsmith had begun to wonder if his imagination had exaggerated the mental picture he'd retained of the beast. Although the sasquatch had its back turned to them and it remained crouched over as it ate, the creature appeared to be just as formidable as Clint had recalled.

The stench of the sasquatch assaulted their nostrils. A heavy stink of musk threatened to choke the four hunters. They fanned out as they approached in order to form a horseshoe formation with Clint and Koduc at each end and Janice and Wardell in the middle.

Less than seventy-five yards from the beast, they were close enough to hear it chomp and chew its food. With uncanny speed, the creature plunged a thick-fingered hand into the pond and plucked a bull frog out of the water. It grunted with satisfaction and stuffed the live frog into its mouth. Bones crunched under the Bigfoot's grinding teeth. Clint felt his stomach ball up in revulsion and fear, but he and the others kept moving closer to their quarry.

Suddenly, the creature stopped eating. Mounds of muscle, visible even beneath the dense dark fur, stiffened. Something had alerted the beast to their presence. Perhaps it had detected a faint sound or an image noticed via peripheral vision or the smell of human fear. The sasquatch slowly began to rise.

Janice was the first to run forward. Wardell, holding

the other end of the net, followed her example. Clint braced his rifle against a hip, prepared to shoot the beast if it became violent. Koduc brought up the rear, fumbling with his rope and the Sharps rifle.

*"Now!"* the girl shouted.

The sasquatch pivoted, its huge body a big dark blur. Janice and Wardell hurled the net with coordination and skill developed by many hours of practice. They'd planned, schemed and trained for this moment. Now it was to be put to the ultimate test.

The creature rose to full height. Over seven feet tall, it towered above its would-be captors. Yet the thrown net sailed over the head of the sasquatch.

A soul-twisting bellow of rage seemed to shake the walls of the ravine as the beast spread its massive arms beneath the net. *It's going to break free*, Clint thought. *That net won't be enough to hold it.*

Reluctantly, the Gunsmith lowered his rifle and unslung the rope from his shoulder. He tossed one end to Janice and together they swung the hemp cord in a high arch over the head of the furious sasquatch. They looped it around the beast and ran in a circle to wind the rope tightly around it.

The creature bellowed again and tried to flee. The net caught underfoot and the giant man-thing crashed to the ground. It howled in anger and thrashed against the bonds which held it fast. Wardell moved in, holding a pole like a lance, prepared to thrust the chloroform-soaked rag into the Bigfoot's face.

"Wait!" Janice yelled, pulling on her end of the rope. "Koduc! We need the other rope! Fast!"

Koduc ran forward and swung his line. The Indian was too frightened to think clearly. He hurled one end of the rope at the struggling giant instead of coordinating the move with one of the others.

Suddenly, one of the beast's arms snaked into view. The sasquatch had ripped through the net. Its arm brushed against the rope and immediately seized it and pulled. Koduc screamed in horror as the sasquatch yanked him forward.

Koduc hurtled past the Bigfoot and plunged headfirst into the pond. The Indian's abrupt dive into the water might have been comical if the situation hadn't been so serious. No one was about to laugh when the giant monster broke free of the net. Clint and Janice released their rope before they too could be yanked forward into the pond—or worse, into the clutches of the sasquatch.

Clint saw the creature's face clearly for the first time. Its small eyes blazed beneath a wide sloped brow. Wide simian nostrils flared and its heavy jaws parted to reveal large teeth with fanglike incisors.

Janice and Wardell, unarmed except for their poles, retreated from the fearsome beast. Clint gathered up the Parker-Hale rifle, not certain himself whether to shoot the sasquatch or not. What if it was human? Primitive, demented, deformed, yet human nonetheless? The creature hadn't attacked them. It only wanted to escape and remain free. The Gunsmith couldn't justify killing the beast for that.

The roar of a gunshot startled Clint. The sasquatch howled in pain and staggered backward. A scarlet stain appeared on its shaggy barrel chest. The beast toppled into the pond like a felled tree. Gallons of water splashed over the shore.

Clint heard the familiar *click-clack* of a lever-action

rifle being cocked. He turned to see Jake Potter and Bison Haggard. The pair stood on the sloped wall of the ravine. The bounty hunter held a Colt revolver in his fist and the mountain man was armed with a Winchester saddle gun.

Both aimed their weapons at the Gunsmith.

# SEVENTEEN

Clint Adams had faced death many times before. He knew from experience when his unbeatable speed and accuracy with a gun could save his life and when it would be an exercise in futility. Even the Gunsmith wasn't fast enough to take two men who already had the drop on him.

He could probably shoot one of them before the two gunmen opened fire. Perhaps he could shoot them both, but unless Potter and Haggard both missed—which wasn't very likely—Clint would die as well.

*The hell with it,* he thought. *I'm going out fighting!*

Suddenly, the pond exploded in a violent thrashing torrent. Koduc screamed and the sasquatch roared. Potter and Haggard turned their attention to the pond. Their jaws dropped open and their eyes bulged with astonishment. Both men swung their weapons toward the water, no longer concerned with the Gunsmith.

"Good Lord!" Wardell exclaimed.

The sasquatch burst from the surface of the water like a hair-covered sea god. It leaped to the shore on the opposite side from its human adversaries. The beast howled, in a sound somewhere between the cry of a lonesome wolf and the wail of a human lunatic. As it ran to the wall of the ravine, it swung a long, clublike object over its head.

Potter and Haggard opened fire on the sasquatch. The Bigfoot moved with incredible speed as it mounted the face of the gully. If any of the shots fired struck the beast, they didn't slow it down. The creature reached the summit of the ravine, turned and hurled its club at the gunmen.

The object sailed over the width of the pond and fell to earth near the feet of Janice Powers and Doctor Wardell. The Englishman gasped and the girl screamed when they stared down at the sasquatch's "club."

It was Koduc's right arm. The limb had been yanked out at the shoulder joint.

The creature roared and angrily slashed its arms in the air before it darted from view and disappeared into the forest. Clint Adams immediately took advantage of the ghastly distraction and swung his Parker-Hale big game rifle at Potter and Haggard.

"Drop your guns!" he ordered, thumbing back the twin hammers of the mighty .60 caliber weapon.

The bounty hunter realized he was no match for the Gunsmith. Potter threw down his revolver and raised his hands in surrender. Haggard lowered his Winchester and glared at Clint.

"I said, *drop it!*" Clint snapped.

The mountain man reluctantly obeyed.

"What about the sasquatch?" Wardell asked.

"It's gone," the Gunsmith replied, keeping his attention and the rifle trained on Potter and Haggard. "We've got two other problems to deal with right now. And I'm looking at both of them."

"Koduc!" Janice cried, rushing to the pond.

"He's dead," Clint told her.

"You can't be sure of that," Wardell began.

"Clint's right, Doctor," Janice announced in a strained, mechanical voice.

She stared into the pond at Koduc's mutilated corpse. The Indian floated face down in the water, now dyed crimson with his blood. The sasquatch had ripped both his arms out of their sockets. The second limb drifted beside the body.

"What are we going to do with these two?" Wardell asked, referring to Haggard and Potter.

"We damn sure can't let them go again," Clint replied.

"You don't intend to kill them, do you?" Janice inquired.

"Not in cold blood," the Gunsmith answered, lowering his rifle. His right hand fell to the modified .45 Colt on his hip. "You two pick up your guns."

The mountain man's eyes widened with alarm, but Jake Potter smiled.

"I ain't gonna do it, Adams," the bounty hunter stated. "And you ain't gonna shoot me neither."

"The hell I won't," Clint told him. "If we don't stop you two now, you'll keep dogging our trail as long as we're in this forest. Even if we don't lead you to the Bigfoot again, you'll try to kill me. That's why I can't let you leave."

"We can tie them up," Wardell suggested.

"Too dangerous," Clint declared. "Haggard is too big and strong and Potter is too damn slippery. He and Crawley were locked away in the local Talo jailhouse and they managed to escape then."

The Gunsmith stepped toward Potter and Haggard. His hand still hovered above the grips of his holstered

Colt. "You fellas have a choice," he said grimly. "Reach for your guns or try to run. Either way, I'll have to kill you both."

Something suddenly hissed through the air as it cut a lightning-quick path from the rim of the ravine. The projectile struck the ground near Clint's feet. Its flint-tipped point sunk into the earth. The thin wooden shaft stood erect, its feathered banner in clear view.

Two more arrows whistled into the gorge and hit the ground near Potter and Haggard. All eyes turned to the top of the ridge where a dozen Huppa braves were stationed. The Indians held drawn bows and lances.

"Throw down weapons, white eyes!" a voice shouted in broken English. "Not throw down, we kill!"

"Now there's a man who knows how to bargain," Clint muttered as he unbuckled his gunbelt and dropped it to the ground.

# EIGHTEEN

The Huppa braves took Clint, Janice, Wardell, Potter and Haggard prisoners. The Indians gathered up the white mans' guns and relieved Haggard of his bowie knife. Then they marched their captives through the forest on foot.

"What about our wagon and horses?" Wardell demanded.

"We not need them," a Huppa Indian replied. "You not need either. Not now."

The remark was ominous enough to silence any further protests from the prisoners.

They soon saw why the Indians had left the vehicle and horses behind. The Huppa escorted their captives into a dense cluster of tangled brush and close-set tree trunks which would have been impossible for a wagon or horses to pass through. Penetrating the foliage was difficult enough on foot. They frequently had to hack through vines and bushes. They were forced to turn sideways to squeeze between tree trunks to keep moving.

Finally, after hours of grueling travel through the merciless terrain, the Huppa led their prisoners to the final destination. A small Indian camp with fourteen tipis, a sweat lodge and a large cage made of wooden bars, was located in a clearing in the heart of the forest.

A handful of Indians met the returning braves and their captives. Most of the tribe who'd remained in the camp were women, children and elderly. The majority of the Huppa kept quite a distance from the prisoners and stared at the white eyes in dumbfounded awe. However, a small, wrinkled old man with long gray hair strode boldly forward to speak with the braves.

The old man wore buckskin clothing, a necklace made of bear teeth and a sash of twisted vine and horse-hair rope. A ceremonial knife, with a blade made of carved ash wood and a mummified deer hoof for a handle, was thrust through the sash. He squinted myopic eyes as he glared at the prisoners. Then he turned to speak to one of the braves in a guttural language unfamiliar to the Gunsmith.

"Jesus, Mary and Joseph," Bison Haggard muttered. "We is purely in shit up to our eyeballs."

"You understand their lingo?" Clint asked.

"Enough to know we got us a ton o' trouble, Adams," the mountain man replied. "This here's their medicine man. I've traded with these Injuns from time to time. His name be Nanho. Young buck he's jawin' with is Tanjo. He's the chief o' this here tribe."

Clint raised his eyebrows. Tanjo was just a kid, no more than eighteen years old. He was tall for a Huppa, about five and a half feet, with a muscular, lean physique and a fierce dark face.

"The ol' chief died a while back," Haggard explained. "Tanjo be his son, so he took over. I've known that boy for a couple years now. He's learned hisself some English from me and other whites what trade with the Huppa, but he ain't real friendly toward none of us. Tanjo is 'bout as close to a warrior as yer likely to find 'mong the Huppa. Reckon he musta got some Cheyenne or Sioux blood in 'im. Never noticed it in his ol' man though.''

"I take it they're upset with us about the sasquatch," Wardell remarked.

"Gawddamn right they is," Haggard snorted. "They's just tryin' to figure out how they's gonna kill us.''

Clint's gaze wandered over the Indian camp, examining the faces of the tribe. Their expressions revealed anger, fear, astonishment and curiosity. However, one young woman seemed more amused than upset or stunned by the presence of the white captives.

She was still in her teens, close to Tanjo's age. The girl's face was round with a wide mouth and big, dark eyes which seemed older than the rest of her features. She wore a simple deerskin dress, provocatively short, with the hem above the knee.

Her eyes met Clint's and she smiled broadly. The Gunsmith grinned in return and nodded at her. *What the hell*, he thought. *If I'm going to die anyway, I might as well flirt a little with this pretty Huppa gal before they kill me.*

"You attacked the *O-Mah*," Tanjo growled, pacing in front of the prisoners. "You shot *O-Mah*. This bad medicine. *O-Mah* forest god. To shoot god bad medicine.''

"Does make sense in a way," Wardell whispered. "If one appreciates the fact these are a primitive people who live—"

"Save it for your lectures, Ed," Clint told him.

"Huppa live their way," Tanjo continued. "*O-Mah* live his way. We both have place in forest. We let each have own way. Live in peace. *O-Mah* strong god in forest, but he not hurt men unless men hurt *O-Mah* first.''

The young chief thrust a finger at his captives. ''You hurt *O-Mah*!'' Tanjo snarled. ''The great medicine man Nanho tells us of a time, long ago, when this happened before. *O-Mah* became a devil god. He seek revenge. This *O-Mah*'s right as forest god. Our medicine can not stop him now. He destroy us all for what you did.''

Bison Haggard stepped forward and spoke to the boy chief in the guttural language of the Huppa. The only words Clint recognized were ''*O-Mah*'' and ''*Huppa*.'' Haggard gestured at Jake Potter, then pointed at the Gunsmith and the two Britons as he spoke.

''You speak our tongue poorly, Hag-gart,'' Tanjo told him. ''Speak English so all know what you speak of them.''

''Ye know me, great chief Tanjo,'' the mountain man replied. ''Ye people have known me for many years. I am a friend to the Huppa and I speak only truth. . . .''

''You not friend of Huppa, Hag-gart!'' Tanjo spat. ''You not man of truth! You speak to save own life!''

''But I do not lie to ye,'' Haggard insisted.

''That is for us to decide,'' the chief declared.

''My brother,'' the pretty Indian girl called to Tanjo. ''The other white eyes know not what Hag-gart says. Should they not be told?''

The chief nodded. ''Lotta is right.'' He faced Clint Adams, Wardell and Janice. ''Hag-gart say you three try to kill *O-Mah*. He and his friend try to stop you.''

''That's a lie,'' Clint hissed. ''I'm sorry I spoke without permission from Chief Tanjo, but I believe in truth and Haggard's lies offend me and make my tongue react before I remember my manners.''

Tanjo nodded with approval at Clint's respect for his position as the leader of the tribe. ''What your name?''

''Clint Adams,'' the Gunsmith replied. ''And I did not shoot the *O-Mah*. Check my rifle and revolver. Both are fully loaded. Smell the barrels. They have not been fired this day.''

He glared at Haggard and Potter. ''Check the guns these two carried. You will find that rounds have been fired from their guns and the barrels smell of burnt powder. They came to kill the *O-Mah*, Chief.''

''Why did you come to forest, Clint Adams?'' Tanjo asked.

''My friends and I also came for the *O-Mah*, that is true,'' the Gunsmith admitted. ''But we came to capture it alive so the medicine men of our people who study the ways of living things could learn about it.''

''White eyes strange people,'' Tanjo remarked. ''Your medicine men want study *O-Mah* to know his way. Why take him from forest that is his home? Why not study him here?''

''That's rather difficult to explain,'' Wardell began.

''They wanted to take the *O-Mah* from the forest so their evil medicine men could change his magic!'' Haggard declared. ''To turn it agin' the Huppa just as the white eyes turned the ol' man Koduc agin' his own people!''

''Koduc!'' Tanjo glared at the Gunsmith. ''I know of Koduc. He turned his face from Huppa long ago when he gave up the way of our gods for white eye's bottle of madness.''

''He guided us through the forest,'' Clint confessed. ''But he—''

"Koduc was man in water with no arms, yes?" Tanjo demanded. "A Huppa has already suffered from anger of *O-Mah*!"

"But Koduc was no longer of your people," Clint said quickly. "You said so yourself!"

"It is not easy to know what we should now do." Tanjo sighed. "I must speak of this with Nanho. We will decide then if you live or die."

# NINETEEN

The prisoners were escorted to the cage and shoved inside. Two Huppa braves armed with lances stood guard by the door which was fastened by a knotted rope of horse hair. The cell was too small for all five captives and they were crowded together like cattle in an undersized pen.

"What a terrible mess we're in!" Wardell exclaimed. "And it's all the fault of you damned bounty hunters!"

"Shut up, Limey!" Potter snapped. "If'n you hadn't come here and stirred up trouble by tellin' everybody that Bigfoot was worth a fortune and all, none of this woulda happened!"

"You blithering idiot!" the Englishman cried. "There is *no reward* offered for the sasquatch! How many times must we tell you that, you stupid, ignorant oaf!"

"Who you callin' stupid?" Potter demanded. "And what the hell is an oaf?"

"Hold on," Haggard began. "Ye say there ain't no bounty for ol' Bigfoot? Potter says—"

"Potter is a moron!" Janice spat.

"You bitch!" Potter snarled. "I know what a moron is!"

"No bloody wonder!" she replied. "Since you've lived with one all your life!"

"Potter," Haggard hissed. "Ye lied to me! Ye got me to guide ye and Crawley a'cause ye promised I'd get me a mighty share of a reward for that critter!"

"Everybody calm down!" the Gunsmith urged, trying to hold Haggard as the mountain man reached for Potter's throat.

"I was gonna get me 'nough money to leave these friggin' woods and set me up a new life somewheres folks won't be knowin' much 'bout me," Haggard growled as he struggled to break free of Clint's grip on his arm. "Now, I learns this regulator bass-turd done give me a tale o' windy. Now, everythin' done been ruined and the Huppa gonna kill us cause o' him!"

"For crissake!" Clint said. "We've got enough problems without fighting among ourselves!"

"Sure, Adams," Potter sneered. "That's why you told the Injuns that Bison and me shot the Bigfoot!"

"Yeah!" Haggard snarled. "Ye done that, Adams! Ye called me a liar too! Ain't no man what does that and lives!"

"Oh, shit," Clint moaned as the mountain man suddenly turned on him.

The muscular Haggard shoved the others against the wooden bars of the cage, bumping into them as he pivoted to grab the Gunsmith's shirtfront. Clint didn't have enough room to throw a decent punch. He jammed an ineffective short right hook into Haggard's ribs which did as much damage as spitting on the burly man.

Haggard seized Clint and rammed him hard into the cage wall. The back of the Gunsmith's head bounced off a spruce wood bar. Haggard slammed him into the cage again and again. Clint clawed at the mountain man's wrists, but he couldn't loosen that iron grip. He rained more abbreviated punches on the brute. The mountain man ignored the feeble blows and continued to dash Clint against the bars.

The others grabbed at Haggard and tried to pull him off the Gunsmith, but the big man was too strong. Janice grasped a fistful of Haggard's beard and tugged hard; he howled and bent backwards giving Clint a chance to throw a solid right to his jaw. The mountain man growled and released him.

"You kill each other?" Tanjo's voice asked. "You save us trouble, white eyes."

The Gunsmith rubbed his aching skull and gazed out at the amused faces of Huppa Indians who had surrounded the cage to watch the fight. The captives finally calmed down, aware that they all shared a mutual problem.

"We're not exactly friends, Chief Tanjo," Clint explained, still rubbing the back of his head.

He suddenly swung his right arm back and slammed the point of his elbow into Haggard's jaw hard enough to knock the mountain man to his knees.

"See what I mean?" he added.

The Indians roared with laughter. Haggard snarled and began to rise, clearly ready to tear Clint apart with his bare hands the same way the sasquatch had killed Koduc. Potter, Wardell and Janice grabbed him. Clint quickly knelt before Haggard and reached inside his shirt to draw the New Line hideout gun.

Using his body and those of the others to conceal the gun from the eyes of the Indian rubberneckers, Clint thrust the diminutive Colt into the throat of the startled mountain man.

"I owed you that rap on the chin, Haggard," Clint whispered. "Now, you behave yourself or I'll kill you right here and now."

The mountain man stared at Clint, amazed that he'd been able to smuggle a gun into the cage. Haggard nodded woodenly. The Gunsmith slid his belly gun into his shirt and turned to face Tanjo.

"Have you decided what to do with us yet?" Clint asked.

"The sweat lodge is to be prepared," Tanjo replied. "Nanho will dream of this matter tonight and he will know what we are to do by dawn."

"Sounds fair," Clint agreed because it wouldn't do any good to say otherwise. "Haggard seems to be going sort of crazy in here. Can you put him somewhere else? Tie him to a tree or something?"

"Why should we care if you kill each other, Clint Adams?" Tanjo asked.

"Because your medicine man has not yet dreamed," the Gunsmith answered.

Tanjo nodded. "We will move Hag-gart."

Clint leaned close to Haggard and whispered, "Before you open your mouth to the chief again, you'd better think about the consequences. We might be able to get out of this mess alive, but not if we keep fighting each other."

"I'm gonna kill ye, Adams," Haggard hissed.

The cell door opened and the mountain man stepped outside. Huppa braves armed with lances escorted him away from the wooden cell.

"But not tonight, you won't." The Gunsmith shrugged.

# TWENTY

Bison Haggard sat at the base of a spruce tree, coils of rope binding him to the thick trunk. Two Huppa stood guard by the mountain man. Haggard glared at the cage where the other prisoners remained. It wasn't difficult to guess which captive he was directing his hateful stare at.

"At least we have more room in here now," Janice remarked as she sat on the dirt floor of the cell.

"Why did you hit Haggard after we finally got him under control?" Wardell asked Clint.

"To make an impression with the Huppa," the Gunsmith replied as he inspected the bars of the cell. "I don't know much about their customs and beliefs, but I figure a tribe that considers a giant hairy beast to be a forest god is apt to admire strength. And Tanjo sure as hell is the type to feel that way. I couldn't let Haggard appear to be the strongest man in our group."

"Well," Potter remarked, "I'm sorta glad we don't have Bison in here with us no more. Feller's plum loco."

"Uh-huh," Clint muttered. "You're not exactly our favorite ally either, Potter."

"I thought we'd agreed to cooperate," Wardell commented. "At least until we can get out of here."

"Yeah," Clint agreed. "Now, let's just figure out how to manage *that* little miracle."

Two Huppa sentries, stationed at the door, watched the prisoners with hard-eyed suspicion. The Indians hadn't charged into the cage to confiscate Clint's New Line Colt, which meant none of them had seen the gun and Haggard hadn't blabbed about it to his captors. In fact, since Wardell, Potter and Janice hadn't asked Clint about the hideout pistol, none of them had noticed it either. The Gunsmith didn't feel obliged to inform them about his belly gun. The fewer the number of people who know about a secret, the longer it remains one.

"How sturdy you figure this cage to be?" Potter asked Clint.

"Well," the Gunsmith began, "they must have put this thing together in a sort of a hurry. Probably figured it might come in handy after they saw us the other day, so they built it just in case. This wood was cut recently. You can tell that from the smell. The bars are just held together by ropes. We could probably manage to undo some of the cords and remove a couple bars and slip right through."

"What about the guards?" Janice asked.

"That's why we're not going to try to escape," Clint answered. "At least, not yet. We'd get a spear in the gut before we moved ten feet from here."

"So we're just going to sit here and let these savages kill us?" Wardell demanded. "That doesn't sound like the sort of advice I'd expect from you, Clint."

"Look, right now, we're okay," the Gunsmith began. "The situation isn't bad enough for desperate action, but it isn't favorable enough for us to try to make a break. Let's just keep a cool head and wait awhile. Maybe a better chance will come along.''

"I figure the odds ain't that bad, Adams," Potter commented. "There's only two guards and they're just armed with spears."

"And those Huppa lances have a greater reach than our arms do, Potter," Clint stated, glad that the bounty hunter didn't know about the .22 hidden under his shirt. "Those fellas have been careful not to get too close to these bars. Jumping them wouldn't be easy. Besides, we'd have to do it silently. If one of them screamed, he'd alert the entire camp. And don't forget the other two sentries stationed by Haggard. They can see us from there and they're too far away to strangle. That's two more spears to deal with and two more mouths that can tell the rest of the tribe we've broken out of this jail."

"Yes," Wardell agreed. "And you know what that forest is like. How far do you think we can get traveling through that sort of dense foliage? The Indians are used to it. They'd catch up with us in a matter of minutes unless we can manage to get a considerable head start."

"So what do you high 'n' mighty thinkers suggest?" Potter growled.

"I figure we'd better hope the medicine rules in our favor," the Gunsmith answered.

At dusk, Nanho entered the sweat lodge. His scrawny, wrinkled body was naked except for the beartooth necklace and his talisman dagger. The prisoners had watched the tribe prepare the lodge. A fire had been built within the structure to heat stones piled in the center.

The lodge was designed to retain heat. The medicine

man would sweat profusely inside the building. Clint wasn't sure why Indians believed this helped a man get mystical guidance, but it was a common practice among numerous tribes throughout America, including some with cultures and customs that were otherwise entirely different, such as the Navajo and the Comanche.

"Actually, the same notion can be found in cultures all over the world," Wardell explained. "Rather hard to say where it all started, but there are similar practices found in the Orient and even in Northern Europe. Some believe a sweat lodge has some sort of medicinal value. It's supposed to be a cure for everything from colds to venereal disease. Others, like our Indian friends, think of it in an occult sense."

"What if the old man just gets sweaty and doesn't have any visions tonight?" Janice asked.

"Oh, he'll have visions," Clint assured her. "Did you see him sitting outside the lodge smoking that long wooden pipe? Well, it didn't have tobacco in the bowl."

"Peyote?" Wardell asked.

"Or locoweed, magic mushrooms or whatever sort of herb they could find that serves the same purpose."

"So the medicine man is going to have hallucinations all night and our fate will depend on the outcome?" Wardell asked, clearly horrified by the situation.

"That's a fact," the Gunsmith confirmed. "We might as well try to get some sleep and wish Nanho sweet dreams."

# TWENTY-ONE

"Are you awake, Clint Adams?" a woman's voice whispered.

The Gunsmith gazed between the bars of the cell and recognized the lovely face of Lotta, the Indian girl.

"Evening, ma'am," he greeted. "Did you bring us some peanuts?"

"Peanuts?" she asked, confused by the remark.

"Reckon I'm still a little groggy," Clint explained quickly. "Not quite awake yet. What can I do for you, ma'am?"

"I wish to talk with you," the girl said.

"You've certainly got a captive audience." He grinned.

"I do not wish to talk here. The guards will untie the gate. Do not try to escape. I warn you, Clint Adams."

"I don't think I'd care to get a Huppa lance in the back trying to run," he replied. "Besides, I've never been one to flee from a pretty lady and I'm a curious fella by nature. I'd like to hear what you've got to say."

The sentries let Clint out of his cage. The Gunsmith wondered if the other prisoners were asleep or merely pretending to be. If it was the latter, Clint mentally congratulated them on their self-control. Most Indians—most people for that matter—admire someone who faces death in a nonchalant manner. Protests, begging and whining wouldn't impress the Huppa, but a display of calm courage would.

Lotta led Clint through the camp, accompanied by an armed guard. They passed by Bison Haggard. The mountain man snored, apparently able to sleep soundly despite the fact that he was bound to a tree trunk and guarded by two Huppa braves.

Clint heard soft chanting as they walked near the sweat lodge; Nanho's voice sounded mournful to the Gunsmith. It could have been the voice of a ghost in a haunted house who wandered the halls at night, searching for a loved one lost to Eternity. Clint didn't understand the language and customs of the Huppa, so he tried not to worry about it.

The Gunsmith followed Lotta to a tipi at the west side of the camp. A Huppa sentry posted himself at the entrance as Clint and Lotta slipped through the flap to enter the tent.

"I guess this is about as private as we can get around here," Clint remarked. "What do you want to talk about, ma'am?"

"Why do you call me *May-um*?" she demanded. "Do you not know my name?"

"You're Lotta," Clint answered. "I addressed you as ma'am to express respect. It is a custom of my people."

"You are with my people now," Lotta stated as she sat on a blanket. "You will call me by my name."

Little light crept into the tipi, but the Gunsmith still saw the girl clearly enough. She sat cross-legged on the blanket. The hem of her buckskin dress rode several inches higher to display plenty of thigh. Clint's manhood began to strain against the crotch of his Levi's.

"Sit with me, Clint Adams," she told him.

"My pleasure, Lotta," he assured her as he joined the girl on the blanket.

"I look upon you with favor," she stated. "A man desires a woman. That is part of nature. A woman desires a man in much the same way."

"I know." Clint grinned. "Personally, I like that arrangement just fine."

"Is it not true white women lack a fire within?" Lotta asked.

"Not the ones I favor," the Gunsmith replied. "You see, my people tend to raise girls not to be too bold with fellas. They're not supposed to seem to be interested in men."

"That is foolish," Lotta commented. "It must be difficult to be a white woman and play such games."

"It can be pretty frustrating to be a white man at times too," Clint told her.

"This custom of your people is stupid, dishonest and wasteful of time that can be better spent. Why do your people have such a custom?"

"I really don't know," Clint admitted. "It'd be okay with me if they threw away that chapter from the social rule book. Still, I've known some gals who don't pay it much mind. White women still have the fire within, believe me."

"Have you had many white women?" Lotta asked.

"Enough to speak from experience," Clint confessed.

"How would you compare me with them?" the Indian girl asked.

"I wouldn't, Lotta," the Gunsmith answered, placing a hand on her leg. "You're one of a kind."

"Is that so?" she inquired, glancing down at his

fingers which slowly stroked her thigh.

"You're beautiful like the breaking of dawn," Clint told her as he removed his hat and placed it on the ground near the blanket. "Yet you express wisdom beyond your years and I admire your honesty. You stir the fire in me as well."

The Gunsmith's gentle touch moved to Lotta's inner thigh. He kissed the girl's face slowly. Clint knew that the romantic customs of the American Indian differed from those of his culture. Some tribes aren't inclined to kiss on the mouth. He wasn't sure how the Huppa regarded this practice, so he didn't rush it.

Clint also took advantage of the opportunity to draw his .22 New Line Colt. He had no intention of using it on the girl, especially since she had indeed stirred a fire inside him. Still, he didn't want her to discover the concealed weapon while they embraced. That could ruin the whole evening. Clint quickly slipped the diminutive pistol from his shirt and hid it under his stetson before using both arms to draw the girl closer.

The situation was strange and sensuous. The Gunsmith was boldly stroking Lotta's breasts and thighs, yet he hesitated to kiss her. The girl responded eagerly enough to Clint's touch. She hiked up her skirt even higher and spread her legs to allow his fingers access to her womanhood. Lotta's hands roamed over Clint's chest and abdomen. She stroked his hardened penis and fumbled with the buttons of his trousers.

Clint pressed his mouth against hers as they lay back on the blanket. His hand moved under her skirt. Lotta wore nothing under the deerskin garment. Clint's fingers probed her womb. His own passion had reached a level that dominated his thoughts and actions. He no longer questioned what Lotta's motives might be for the meeting. The Gunsmith wanted her—plain and simple.

Lotta smiled when she saw Clint unbuckle his belt. She turned over and positioned herself on hands and knees. Clint watched the girl reach back to yank her skirt up over the curves of her buttocks. He hastily pulled down his pants and accepted the unspoken invitation.

The Gunsmith knelt between her legs and stroked the smooth, soft skin on her rump. His hand slithered between her thighs, finding the warm, wet portal of love. Lotta moaned with pleasure as Clint's hand moved back and forth. Her body began to rock with the motion.

Clint removed his fingers and guided his hard, swollen cock into the center of her womanhood. Lotta sighed happily and wiggled her bottom against his abdomen, working him deeper. Clint's hips jerked to and fro to assist in the penetration. His hands stroked Lotta's buttocks and thighs as he began to thrust.

The girl groaned and began vibrating faster. Clint rammed himself into her again and again. Lotta hammered a fist into the ground in wild passion, fearing to cry out within the camp. Clint drove himself deeper, faster. Lotta's head thrashed from side to side as she convulsed in an uncontrollable orgasm.

Clint let her rest for less than a minute before he continued driving his manhood into her love chamber. The girl whimpered and squealed, but her body kept bucking and bouncing vigorously. Clint gripped her hips and thrust with all his might.

''Ahhh!'' Lotta cried, unable to restrain herself any longer.

The Gunsmith gasped as his organ exploded, finally

releasing its hot seed into her quivering flesh. Lotta collapsed on the blanket, breathing hard. Clint lay beside her, taking the girl in his arms.

"Why did you do that?" she whispered.

The Gunsmith was startled and a little worried by the question. "Because I wanted you and I thought you felt the same."

"Yes," Lotta admitted, apparently satisfied with his answer." I will talk to my brother, but I do not promise I can save your life tomorrow."

Clint briefly considered his odds for an escape from the Huppa camp. Although he'd hate to use his fist on the pretty Indian girl's face, he could render her unconscious, tear a hole in the tipi and slip away into the night. The Gunsmith would have a good chance of getting away, but he'd be forced to abandon Dr. Wardell and Janice Powers.

He still had the little .22 Colt, but that wouldn't help him silently dispatch the sentries. He might have considered creeping up from behind and slugging the guards or threatening them at gunpoint if he didn't have to deal with two separate pairs of sentries within clear view of each other. There was no way he could free Janice and Wardell without resorting to shooting—and a short-barreled .22 revolver would be a sorry weapon to take on a dozen skilled archers with.

"If I have to die tomorrow," Clint told Lotta as he stroked her flesh, "let us spend tonight knowing life."

# TWENTY-TWO

Clint Adams returned to the cage three hours later. Potter and Janice were sound asleep. Edward Wardell glanced up at the Gunsmith and smiled thinly.

"Glad to see you returned in one piece," he whispered.

"Yeah," Clint replied. "We might have an ally in the Huppa camp. Lotta said she'd try to convince her brother that we didn't mean to harm the *O-Mah*."

"You must have made quite an impression on her," Wardell said dryly.

"I just hope she makes an impression on Tanjo when she pleads our case."

Clint sat down on the ground and propped his back against the bars. Tilting the brim of his stetson over his eyes, the Gunsmith relaxed and drifted into a shallow slumber. There was nothing he could do until morning. Perhaps he'd die tomorrow, but that was something the Gunsmith had learned to accept long ago. Death was inevitable for all men—but it would wait until tomorrow.

At dawn, the medicine man emerged from the sweat lodge. Nanho walked unsteadily, his shriveled body damp and trembling. Huppa braves draped a fur robe around the old man's shoulders. Tanjo approached Nanho. Together, they moved to the young chief's tipi.

"Well, the jury is deliberating." Wardell remarked.

"No jury," Clint corrected. "Just a couple of judges."

"Yeah," Potter muttered. "And we can guess what the verdict is gonna be."

"We're not dead yet," Janice said. Her tone sounded less optimistic than her words.

"Wait a few minutes," Potter replied glumly.

The bounty hunter was wrong. Tanjo and Nanho didn't emerge from the tipi until an hour later. When they stepped outside, Lotta met the pair and spoke to them. All three returned to the tipi for another conference.

"Well, our lawyer has arrived," Wardell mused.

"What?" Janice blinked, confused by his remark.

"I'll explain later," Clint told her—hoping he wouldn't have to.

Finally, Tanjo, Nanho and Lotta emerged from the tipi and approached the cage. The chief uttered a curt order in his native tongue and the sentries unfastened the cord that bound the cell door.

"Here we go," Clint rasped.

The prisoners stepped outside. Bison Haggard was also freed from the bonds that held him to the tree. The mountain man stomped forward, glaring at the Gunsmith.

"Tanjo," he growled. "I got me a request. If'n yer gonna kill us all anyways, let me take care of Adams personal-like afore ye kill me."

"The gods have told us what must be done," Tanjo replied. "And it is for us to carry out their will."

The chief turned to face Clint Adams and the others. "My sister tells me you claim you and the two Englanders came to capture the *O-Mah*."

"That's true," Clint admitted.

"But you did not intend to kill the forest god?" Tanjo asked.

"Like I told you yesterday," the Gunsmith answered, "we came to take the *O-Mah* away to study it. We meant it no harm."

"The *O-Mah* is not to leave the forest." Tanjo frowned. "The gods look upon your actions without favor."

"We realize that now." The Gunsmith nodded. "And it was a mistake for us to try to capture the *O-Mah*. Its place is here in the woods. . . ."

"Hold on, Clint—" Wardell began.

"Edward." Clint rolled his eyes. *"Don't argue!"*

"Then you will not seek the *O-Mah* again?" Tanjo inquired. "You will not try to take him from his home?"

"No," Clint replied.

"I want the Englander's word of this as well."

"Oh, well." Wardell sighed. "We won't hunt the *O-Mah* again. You have my word."

"That is good." Tanjo nodded. "But the *O-Mah* was shot by one of you."

"Yes," Clint confirmed. "Haggard and Potter shot the *O-Mah*. None of my friends harmed it."

"Yer a liar, Adams!" Haggard snarled. "I done said that afore. Ye tried to tell the Huppa me and Potter shot the *O-Mah*, but ye know damn good 'n' well we was tryin' to drive ye away from the forest gawd to protect everybody from the *O-Mah*'s curse."

"Then why had your guns been fired and mine

hadn't been?'' Clint demanded.

" 'Cause the rifle ye used to shoot the *O-Mah* was drawn from yer hand by the magic of the forest gawd,'' Haggard answered. "We seen the gun float through the air, aglowin' like a hot coal in a campfire. Then it fell to the water and hissed like a red-heated horseshoe. It's still at the bottom o' that pond, 'long with the body of the Huppa traitor what brung ye.''

"Hell, Haggard.'' The Gunsmith snorted. "You had all night to dream up a story and that bullshit fairy tale is the best you could come up with?''

"The magic of the *O-Mah* is well known to my people,'' Chief Tanjo said grimly. "Hag-gart might speak truth.''

"Truth is stronger than lies, ain't that so?'' the mountain man demanded.

"Truth has the strength of the gods,'' Tanjo replied. "All things of nature are truth. Gentle or hard, fruitful or barren, life and death are all truth. Lies are a device of men.''

"Then the gods will be with the feller what speaks the truth,'' Haggard stated. "So what say ye put me and Adams to a test? Truth against lies?''

"You speak of trial by combat, Hag-gart?'' Tanjo inquired.

"Hand to hand.'' The mountain man nodded. "We'll fight without weapons.''

"With your bare hands?'' Tanjo asked.

"Oh, shit!'' Clint rasped, staring at Haggard's six foot six, muscular frame.

"That be fine by me,'' Haggard agreed.

"Clint Adams,'' Tanjo began, "what do you say to this contest?''

"Haggard's a lot bigger than I am,'' the Gunsmith

replied. "He'd naturally have an advantage in a bare-handed battle."

"The gods' strength will be with the man who represents truth," the chief insisted. "You should have no need to fear unless you lie."

"Uh, sure," Clint answered. "I just figured I should point out how Haggard is bigger than I am so you'll all realize how strong my truth is when I whip him."

"Then let the contest begin," Chief Tanjo declared. "And let the fight be to the death."

# TWENTY-THREE

"Take this," Clint whispered to Edward Wardell as he slipped the .22 New Line Colt to the archaeologist, using their bodies for a shield to conceal the gun from the eyes of the Huppa.

"My word . . . ." Wardell gasped.

"Just take it and hide it inside your shirt," Clint urged. "*Fast!*"

The Gunsmith then moved to the center of the camp. Bison Haggard stood waiting for his opponent. The mountain man grinned confidently as he flexed his thick fingers, eager to begin the bare-handed contest. The Indians formed a circle around the combatants, clearing a wide area for the unarmed duel.

"Hold on!" Haggard shouted, thrusting a finger at Clint. "That bass-turd done got him a gun tucked inside his shirt!"

Tanjo turned sharply and glared at the Gunsmith. Several braves notched arrows to bowstrings and prepared to draw back their weapons to open fire. Clint Adams dramatically ripped off his shirt with exaggerated outrage.

"See!" he shouted. "I carry no weapons! Haggard again lies! Does he now lie because he hesitates to fight me on equal terms? Is he a coward as well as a liar?"

"Why ye son of a diseased slut!" the mountain man

snarled. ''I'll break yer friggin' back over my knee like it was a gawddamn stick!''

''Gonna talk me to death, Haggard?'' Clint sneered.

The big man bellowed in pure bestial rage and charged, his powerful arms outstretched, fingers arched like the talons of a bird of prey. The Gunsmith had purposely goaded Haggard, hoping to make him angry. When a man loses his temper, he tends to become careless. Clint hoped his opponent got plenty careless. Otherwise, Bison Haggard would probably tear him apart.

The Gunsmith waited until Haggard was almost upon him before he moved. Clint sidestepped out of the mountain man's path and simultaneously hurled his shirt at Haggard's face. The trick worked better than Clint had dared hope. His shirt dropped neatly over Haggard's head like a hood.

The big man's growl contained a puzzled sound and he stumbled awkwardly to come to an abrupt halt. Clint moved in quickly, lashing a boot into the other man's groin. Haggard groaned and doubled up. Clint's left arm snaked around the mountain man's neck. The headlock pinned down the shirt which was still draped over Haggard's head. Clint's right fist slammed into the hooded face twice. Blood seeped through the cloth of the shirt.

Suddenly, Haggard straightened his back and scooped up the startled Gunsmith. The big man roared as he slung Clint across his shoulder and spun him around before hurling the Gunsmith like a bale of hay. Clint crashed to the earth.

The breath spewed from his lungs; his backbone seemed to be cracked, sending shards of pain dancing through his body. Lights exploded before Clint's eyes.

He blinked desperately, trying to clear his vision as the towering figure of Bison Haggard approached.

Clint saw the mountain man raise a booted foot. The Gunsmith rolled aside, narrowly avoiding a murderous stomp. Haggard's other foot swung forward and Clint jerked his head aside. The boot stamped into the ground next to Clint's right ear.

Haggard growled like a bear, frustrated by Clint's evasive actions. He finally reached down to grab the Gunsmith. Clint rolled onto his shoulders and powered both legs in a high kick. The twin boot heels slammed into Haggard's face.

The mountain man staggered backward, blood flowing from his split lips and both nostrils. Clint quickly scrambled to his feet and faced his opponent.

"That's how it's done, dumb ass," he stated.

Haggard bellowed and charged once more. Again, Clint did the unexpected. He also lunged forward and dove to the ground to roll into his adversary's legs. The mountain man tripped as Clint's body clipped him at the shins. Haggard fell headlong to the dust.

Clint jumped up and rushed forward to deliver a kick to Haggard's shaggy skull. His boot tagged the mountain man on a shoulder. Suddenly, Haggard shot up to his feet, his face a bloodied mask of rage.

A big fist slammed into Clint's stomach. The Gunsmith's body jackknifed from the blow, but he managed to raise a forearm to block Haggard's next punch. Clint countered with an uppercut to the larger man's testicles.

Haggard howled in agony and began to double up. Clint pivoted and reached back to snare the mountain man's hairy head with both arms. Then he dropped to one knee and hauled the big man over his shoulder.

Haggard slammed forcibly to the ground.

Clint hammered the bottom of his fist into the bridge of Haggard's nose before he scurried away to avoid the big man's slashing hands and feet. Bison Haggard slowly rose to his feet, blood oozing from his broken, mashed-in nose. His eyes were glazed and he walked unsteadily on weak legs, but still he advanced.

The Gunsmith had gained the upper hand in the brutal contest, but he mentally warned himself not to underestimate Haggard. The mountain man had already taken enough punishment to put three ordinary men out of action and he was still on his feet. *Don't get overconfident*, Clint thought. *But end it quickly. This guy's got more stamina than a bull moose. If he gets enough time to get his second wind, he'll be swinging at me as hard as before.*

Clint raised a boot and feinted a kick for Haggard's groin. The mountain man's hands dropped to protect his crotch, leaving his face wide open to attack. Clint hit him with a right cross, followed by a left hook.

Haggard swung a wild roundhouse punch. Clint ducked under the attacking arm and came up with a left jab to the point of his opponent's bearded chin. Haggard's head snapped back from the blow and Clint slammed his right fist into the mountain man's jaw as hard as he could. He felt the recoil ride through his arm to the shoulder when the punch connected. Bison Haggard's eyes crossed as he dropped to his knees. Then he crashed, face first, to the ground.

Clint Adams staggered away from his vanquished opponent. Chief Tanjo strode forward and pointed at Haggard's unconscious body.

"The battle is to be to the death," he stated.

"Haggard asked for the fight, but I won, so I'm not

obliged to meet his terms," Clint replied breathlessly. "Besides, he has wronged your people. I will not deny you the right to punish him."

"So be it." Tanjo nodded.

Before he could announce the final judgment for all the captives, a horrible wail—neither animal nor human—erupted from the forest. Everyone stood rooted to the ground. Fear traveled through their spinal cords like icy needles.

"*O-Mah!*" Nanho the medicine man whispered, his eyes wide with terror.

# TWENTY-FOUR

A rock as big as a horse's head hurled from the trees as if propelled from a catapult. It smashed into a tipi. Skins and framework collapsed and the tent fell in ruin. The Huppa cried out in alarm and despair as a huge, dark shape emerged from the treeline.

The sasquatch stood at the perimeter of the camp, holding another boulder in its large gnarled hands. Dried blood formed a rust-colored crust on the hairs of its chest. Its mouth was contorted in a frozen snarl, white foamy spittle dripping from its parted jaws.

The beast suddenly raised the stone overhead and hurled it at the congregation in the center of the camp. Frightened Huppa ran in all directions. One didn't move fast enough. The rock smashed into the brave's chest and crushed him like an insect.

"Good Lord!" Edward Wardell exclaimed. "What are we going to do now?"

"That's obvious," Clint Adams replied. "Run like hell!"

The sasquatch charged into the camp. Huppa braves, reluctant to attack a creature they regarded as a supernatural forest god, held their lances and bows defensively in front of them, yet refused to launch a weapon at the towering beast.

The *O-Mah* reached out, seized one man's spear

and yanked the hapless brave forward. It clamped its free hand around the Indian's throat and raised him until the man's feet were several inches above the ground. The Huppa brave thrashed wildly in the beast's grasp as it strangled him to death. The sasquatch tossed the man's corpse and the spear aside. It continued to march into the camp.

Janice Powers handed Clint his shirt. The Gunsmith rapidly slid his arms into it, watching the Bigfoot turn its fury on another tipi. The powerful creature ripped the tent apart, scattering poles and torn cloth with its lashing arms.

"Head for the forest," Clint ordered, pointing to the east. "Over there. Hide in the brush and wait for me."

"What are you going to—" Wardell began.

"Wait three minutes," Clint interrupted. "If I'm not back by then, go on without me."

The two Britons and Jake Potter dashed for the trees while the Gunsmith galloped to the chief's tipi. The sasquatch still roared and Huppa cried out helplessly as the beast rampaged through the camp.

Clint entered Tanjo's tent to find the young chief was already inside. Tanjo stood in the center of the tipi with Clint's gunbelt in his hands. Tanjo glared at the Gunsmith as he grabbed the butt of the modified Colt.

"You did this to us, white eyes!" Tanjo snapped, yanking the gun from its holster.

The Gunsmith lunged forward and caught Tanjo's wrist behind the pistol. His fist crashed into the chief's jaw and Tanjo's knees buckled. Clint twisted the Colt from his grasp.

Tanjo sprang back with surprising strength and seized Clint's wrists, trying to wrestle the revolver from him. The Gunsmith butted his forehead into the chief's face and followed up with a left hook which knocked him to all fours. Clint clipped Tanjo behind the ear with the barrel of his Colt and the chief fell unconscious.

"Sorry, kid," the Gunsmith muttered as he buckled on his gunbelt. "You've got your customs and I've got mine—and staying alive is one I take sort of personal."

He located his Parker-Hale rifle and immediately bolted from the tipi. A Huppa brave tumbled across the ground in front of Clint. The Indian's face had been smashed into crimson pulp.

The sasquatch sent another Huppa sprawling with a violent swipe of its powerful arm. Other Indians fled from the beast. A couple of braves overcame their superstitious fear of the *O-Mah* and fired arrows at the creature, but their hands trembled so badly every missile missed the rapidly moving forest giant.

Clint didn't have time to witness any further destruction delivered by the sasquatch. He ran to the treeline and plunged into the forest. Clint found Janice, Wardell and Potter crouched behind some bushes. They were pale and frightened, but they'd escaped unharmed.

"Okay," the Gunsmith began, "let's get out of here."

"What about the Indians?" Janice asked. "We shouldn't just leave them to be slaughtered by the sasquatch."

"What can we do?" Clint demanded. "We're on the Huppa shit list. I didn't shoot that thing because the Huppa would still want our blood even if we killed the Bigfoot. They'd blame us for the monster going on the rampage . . . and maybe *they'd be right*!"

"Hell, Adams," Potter snorted. "Ain't our fault

that critter decided to rip up the Injun village. . . .''

"But why did it go berserk, Potter?" Clint asked angrily. "It's because you and that other idiot Haggard shot it!"

"That's right," Janice agreed. "The wound has obviously become infected. The pain has driven the animal insane. It's not uncommon for a wounded animal to react in such a violent manner after being wounded. Once in Rhodesia, an elephant with a broken piece of tusk lodged in the roof of its mouth ran amok—"

"I think we've got the idea, Janice." Wardell sighed. "I suppose we'll have to give up trying to catch the sasquatch now."

"Edward," Clint growled, "don't even *think* about that!"

# TWENTY-FIVE

The Gunsmith, Janice, Wardell and Potter fought their way through the dense brush. Thorns and branches ripped their clothes and cut their hands, but the sound of the roaring sasquatch and the horrified wailing of Huppa Indians urged them to keep moving.

"Do you think the Huppa will follow us?" Edward Wardell asked breathlessly as he squeezed himself between two close-set spruce trees.

"I wouldn't be surprised," the Gunsmith replied. "And they won't take us prisoner again. They'll simply kills us if they get the chance."

"I sorta figure they'll be satisfied after they cut up Haggard for shootin' the Bigfoot," Potter remarked.

"I doubt it," Clint said. "I had to cold-cock the chief when I went back for my guns."

"That's apt to get them upset with us," Janice agreed. She was keeping up with the men well. In fact, she was holding her own better than Wardell.

"Yeah, Adams," Potter muttered. "I notice you didn't bother to get my guns while you was at it."

"You want your guns?" Clint replied. "Go back and get them yourself. I don't trust you enough to give you a firearm, Potter. Just be happy we let you come along with us. You haven't given us any reason to welcome your company, fella."

"Hell, Adams." The bounty hunter shrugged. "I was just tryin' to make a dollar or two, same as you."

"Not the same as me, regulator." Clint sneered. "I didn't join this expedition for money."

"Why did you decide to join us?" Wardell asked. "After all, you're not a scientist. I never did quite understand your reason. I was just glad you came along."

"Bloody lucky for us he did," Janice added.

"Do mind your language, dear," the Englishman told her.

"How come you Limeys figure 'bloody' is such an awful word?" Potter inquired.

"It refers to 'blood of the Virgin,' if you must know," Wardell answered. "And don't ask which virgin. Even you should be able to figure that out."

" 'Course I know what you mean," the bounty hunter sniveled. "I'll have you know my daddy was a preacherman back in Arkansas."

"I'm certain he's very proud of you," Janice said dryly.

"You reckon so?" Potter asked. Her sarcasm had fluttered over his head unnoticed. "I always figured he might not understand too good. . . ."

The Gunsmith rolled his eyes, exasperated by Potter's stupidity. The conversation had wandered from Wardell's question about why Clint had joined the expedition and he didn't really care to try to explain it anyway. He wasn't sure of the reason himself.

Perhaps his reason had been curiosity, a trait which had always been a major part of the Gunsmith's personality—and, as often as not, it had gotten him into trouble. The sasquatch hunt hadn't been an exception to that rule.

However, Clint's curiosity had been satisfied enough for his taste. Maybe science would never accept the sasquatch, but Clint had all the proof he needed. He wanted to get away from the forests of Northern California, the domain of the Huppa and Bigfoot.

"Say," Wardell began, "we are heading back to the wagon and our supplies, aren't we?"

"Yeah," Clint replied. "Wouldn't make much sense to go anywhere else, would it?"

"No," the Englishman agreed. "I suppose not."

"Listen!" Janice urged.

Everyone fell silent. Potter whispered, "I don't hear nothin'."

"That's the point," Clint explained. "The Bigfoot must have finished tearing up the Huppa village. It isn't roaring in anger anymore and the Indians are quiet too."

"Perhaps we're out of earshot of the village," Wardell suggested.

"Not this soon," Clint replied. "But we'd better keep going, at least until sunset. I doubt if the Huppa will want to try tracking us after dark—not with the sasquatch on the rampage."

"Maybe they killed the son of a bitch," Potter mused.

"I wouldn't bet on that," the Gunsmith told him. "Those braves were so scared of Bigfoot most of them wouldn't lift a finger to defend themselves against it. The few that tried were so nervous when they fired arrows or threw lances they couldn't have hit the side of a mountain."

"They might not have to kill it," Janice said. "The beast will eventually bleed to death. It's just a question of how badly it's been hurt internally and how strong its constitution is.''

"Sure as shit didn't seem weak and feeble to me," Potter remarked.

"True." Janice nodded. "But running amok like that will only increase the creature's bleeding. Of course, since we don't know enough about the animal's anatomy or the extent of its injuries, there's no way of judging how long it will take to die.''

"Indeed," Wardell agreed. "It might take an hour or it might take several days before the creature finally goes into shock and dies.''

"What puzzles me," Clint said, "is why did it attack the Huppa village? It didn't seem like a violent animal until Potter and Haggard wounded it. Even when the sasquatch killed Koduc, it was acting in self-defense. Why seek out the village and attack it?''

"I'm certain that was a coincidence," Wardell stated. "The village just happened to be available when the beast went berserk.''

"Maybe," Clint answered. "But there may have been another reason.''

"Really?" The Englishman raised an eyebrow at Clint. "What?''

"Revenge.''

"On the Huppa?" a confused Potter asked.

"On us," Clint said. "After all, from Bigfoot's point of view it would sure seem that all of us were working together when we attacked him at the pond. . . .''

"It wasn't an attack," Wardell insisted.

"But it might well seem to be to the sasquatch," Janice said.

"What if the creature is intelligent enough to realize

it's dying?'' the Gunsmith continued. ''It could also figure out we were responsible and then track us to the Huppa village and destroy the Indian camp for protecting us.''

''They took us prisoner, damn it!'' Potter spat.

''The Bigfoot wouldn't know that,'' Clint said. ''I'm just wondering—if that thing's still alive, will it come after us again?''

# TWENTY-SIX

Twilight descended and the Gunsmith's group finally rested after hours of fighting their way through the formidable brush of the forest. They sat on the ground, bone weary from their ordeal. Wardell, Potter and Janice were so exhausted, they nearly drifted off to sleep until the Gunsmith reminded them of the danger that remained.

"We can't rest for long. We'll have to keep going until we reach the wagon."

"Jesus, Adams," Potter complained. "In the dark we could wind up wanderin' off in the wrong direction if'n we go on now."

"That won't happen if everybody stays together and nobody panics," Clint insisted. "We can't afford to rest any longer. The Huppa could be on our trail already and they'll damn sure start tracking us in the morning. They're used to this California jungle and they're better at reading sign than we are. It won't take them long to catch up with us if we don't keep moving."

"Well, at least we'll be able to have a decent meal when we get to our supplies," Wardell said as he rose to his feet. "I wish those damn Indians had fed us something besides cornmeal and dried fish. We haven't had any proper food for almost two days."

"I know what you mean," Clint agreed. "My stomach is growling too. All the more reason to keep—"

The unexpected report of a rifle startled them. Clint threw himself to the ground and assumed a prone position, the Parker-Hale rifle at the ready. The others scrambled for cover as three more shots echoed through the forest.

Clint heard bullets smack into tree trunks and splinter bark, but his eyes and ears concentrated on locating their assailant. He saw the muzzle flash of a weapon among the trees to the west, but he held his fire. The British big game rifle only held two rounds and the sniper was too far away to use a pistol.

"Hide if'n ye want!" a familiar voice shouted. "I'll find ye!"

"Hell," Potter rasped. "It's Bison! I figured he was a goner for sure!"

"Haggard obviously regained consciousness and managed to avoid both the Huppa and the sasquatch," Wardell remarked.

"And he must have gone into the chief's tipi," Clint added, "and found Potter's Winchester."

"Hey, Adams!" Haggard's voice called. "Ye whupped me pretty good! Didn't figure ye could do it! Where'd ye learn how to fight like that?"

"You were easy, Haggard!" Clint shouted. "The only thing hard about fighting you was having to smell your stink while I beat on your empty head!"

The Gunsmith immediately scrambled to a new position behind a thick spruce tree after delivering his insults. Haggard's rifle boomed twice more and bullets whined as they struck the ground where Clint had been.

"Crap," Clint hissed through his teeth when he saw the muzzle flash of the sniper's weapon. Haggard had changed position as well.

"Tryin' to get me riled again like ye done afore, ain't ye?" Haggard laughed. "That's how ye whupped me back thar at the village. I ain't gonna make that mistake again, Adams!"

"Bison!" the bounty hunter yelled. "It's me! Potter! Don't be a damn fool, Bison! We gotta stick together if'n we wanta come outta this—"

A bullet smashed into a tree trunk Potter was using for cover. Wood chips pelted the regulator's face and he cried out in alarm as he fell flat behind his shelter.

"Ye bass-turds run out on me back there!" the mountain man bellowed. "Ye left me at the mercy of the *O-Mah* and the Huppa! Don't talk none to me 'bout stickin' together, ye snake in the grass bounty hunter!"

The Gunsmith had seen the muzzle flash of Haggard's rifle and noticed it had come from a different position again. Haggard was moving in a circle from the northwest. If Clint could estimate the general area of the man's next position, he might be able to nail him when the mountain man fired again.

"You were willing to let us take the blame for what you did, Haggard!" Clint declared. "Don't bitch to us about loyalty!"

The Gunsmith slithered to another position and aimed his rifle at the spot where Haggard was most likely to move. The mountain man didn't open fire.

"No sense in me burnin' up all my ammo," Haggard said with a laugh. "I know this here forest. Ye don't! I've got all night to pick ye off!"

"All you can pick is your nose, Haggard!" Clint shouted. "That might not feel so good since I broke it for you, huh?"

"Keep talkin', Adams!" the mountain man replied. "Ye make it all the more fun when I kill ye!"

"For crissake, Adams!" Potter rasped. "Gimme a gun!"

"Hey, gal!" Haggard laughed. "Ye act like a snotty high 'n' mighty bitch afore now. Bet ye be willin' to spread yore legs for ol' Bison now!"

"I'd sooner copulate with a dogface baboon, you filthy great bleeder!" Janice screamed back at him.

"Yer gonna do the bleedin', slut!" the mountain man snarled. "Ye 'n' them sons of bitches with ye!"

"You can't even scare a woman, you walking dung heap!" Clint taunted, trying to get Haggard to reveal his position or at least exhaust his ammunition.

"Ye be the dung heap, Adams!" the mountain man shouted. "I'm gonna gut-shoot ye and piss in yore face while yer bleedin' to—"

The final word was followed by a scream which became a cry of agony and terror. The sound of bestial roaring accompanied Haggard's shrieks as bodies thrashed wildly among the shadows.

"My God!" Wardell gasped. "It's the sasquatch!"

"We've got to kill it," Clint said in a tense voice. Moving as rapidly as possible through the brush, he rushed toward the sound of the snarling beast. Clint held the rifle ready, straining his eyes to try to peer into the blackness.

"Clint!" Janice cried. "For God's sake, don't leave us!"

"Follow me!" Clint replied. "Stay close together!"

A patch of moonlight penetrated the roof of branches and leaves overhead. Clint could see a huge, dark shape moving to the east; its size left no doubt as to its identity.

The Gunsmith swung the Parker-Hale buttstock to his shoulder and aimed at the retreating form of the sasquatch. He squeezed the trigger and the big rifle bellowed like a deep-throated cannon.

The recoil was incredible, driving the butt painfully into Clint's shoulder. The rifle climbed high, raising Clint's arms, the twin muzzles pointing at the night sky. The stench of burnt gunpowder filled Clint's nostrils and the orange glare of the muzzle flash illuminated the forest for a fraction of a second.

The Gunsmith lowered the big game gun, his right arm throbbing from the violent kick of the .60 caliber weapon. He heard the bone-chilling cry of the sasquatch in the distance. The creature had already fled beyond Clint's view.

"Did you hit it?" Janice asked as she appeared beside the Gunsmith.

"I'm not sure," Clint confessed. "It didn't go down, so I didn't hit it well enough if I hit it at all."

"Jesus, Adams," Potter said, joining them. "That gun must pack a wallop like a howitzer! If you hit that thing, it'd *have* to come down!"

"You're probably right," Clint was forced to admit. "It's too dark to be sure and I didn't have a clear shot at Bigfoot. That goddamn monster moves so fast you blink and it's half a mile away."

"What about Haggard?" Wardell inquired.

"It's so dark you can't hardly see a damn thing . . ." Potter began.

"What's that?" Janice asked, pointing at a twisted metallic tube on the ground.

Potter picked up the object. It was part of a Winchester rifle with the stock snapped off. The barrel had been bent and deformed into a crooked U shape.

"Jesus, Mary and Joseph!" the bounty hunter whispered. "Bigfoot done broke this gun in two!"

"It did the same to Haggard," Clint Adams added.

He had just discovered the mountain man's corpse draped over a log. The sasquatch had broken Bison Haggard's back.

# TWENTY-SEVEN

"Bison Haggard was stronger than any man I ever met," Potter said, staring at the dead man in amazement. "Never would have believed no critter could do this to him."

"Believe it," Clint Adams muttered as he inspected the corpse.

"What are you doing, Clint?" Janice asked.

"Robbin' the dead, Adams?" the bounty hunter grunted. "Gonna split whatever you find with the rest of us?"

"Shut your mouth, Potter," the Gunsmith replied gruffly. "I was checking to see if Haggard had any weapons, food or matches on him."

"I got matches," Potter said.

"So do I. But you can't have too many in a situation like this."

"I wonder if *anyone* has ever experienced a situation like this," Janice wondered aloud. "Being stalked by an inhuman beast in a forest as impenetrable as any African jungle."

"It has indeed happened before," Wardell announced as he marched forward, holding a torch in his fist. The flame illuminated his face, revealing a wiry grin which surprised the others. "Thousands of years ago, our prehistoric ancestors had to deal with a variety of wild beasts, but man survived''—the Englishman gestured with the torch—''and this is the reason. Fire!''

"Of course!" Janice exclaimed. "The beast might not be frightened of men, but it will certainly fear fire. That's why you're searching Haggard's body for more matches, isn't it, Clint?"

"Yeah," the Gunsmith answered as he rose, "but he doesn't have anything in his pockets we can use."

"Won't fire make us mighty easy to spot if 'n them Indians are trackin' us?"

"Haggard found us so the Huppa would have too," Clint declared, "if they were stalking us by night. That means the only thing we have to worry about is Bigfoot. We can use the torches. It'll help us to see where the hell we're going and it might discourage the sasquatch from coming after us."

"I'd rather have a gun," Potter said glumly.

"So pick up what's left of Haggard's Winchester," Clint shrugged.

"Thanks a lot, Adams."

"Speaking of shooting," Wardell said, "I found a tree trunk over there with a devil of a large chunk ripped out of it. I'd say that's what you shot, Clint."

"Figures." Clint sighed. "That Parker-Hale kicks like it was designed to break a fella's shoulder. I'm not used to the damn thing and I'm not sure I want to go through the pain and discomfort needed to master it."

"Was there any blood?" Janice asked Wardell.

"None that I saw," the Englishman replied. "If the sasquatch is bleeding to death, it's certainly taking its time about it."

"Let's keep moving," the Gunsmith advised. "The sooner we get to the wagon and Duke, the sooner we can get out of this damn forest.''

They continued their grueling trek through the brush. Wardell and Potter carried torches which assisted the group with the additional light. It helped ease their fear as well; terror is always magnified by darkness.

The flames were a problem, however. They had to avoid setting the bushes on fire, which wasn't easy in the thick foliage. The only way to keep the sticks burning was to tear off strips from their shirts and wrap the cloth around the heads of the torches.

Long minutes crept by as they traveled. The Gunsmith worried about Duke. His prize gelding had been left alone and uncared for since the Huppa had taken them captive two days ago. Duke was too well-trained to wander off and smart enough to avoid trouble— unless the Gunsmith got him into it. Still, Clint couldn't help fretting about his horse.

Hours later, they reached the ravine where they had first encountered the sasquatch. Koduc's body still floated in the pond below. Janice gazed down at the Indian's corpse and shook her head.

"We shouldn't leave him like that," she said. "He deserves a decent burial."

"There isn't time, dear," Wardell told her. "I'm certain Koduc would understand."

"It just seems so uncivilized," she stated.

"This whole business has been uncivilized from the start," Clint Adams remarked. "It's been more primitive and savage than anything I've experienced before and I'd just as soon never go through anything like this again."

"Me and you both," Potter added. "Hey, when we

get to the wagon and horses, what say we head west to Yreka?''

"Talo is closer," the Gunsmith remarked.

The bounty hunter shrugged. "Look, maybe you'll help me find my hoss and then we'll split up. How's that sound?''

"We'll talk about it later," Clint said.

The Gunsmith moved away from Potter and stepped close to Edward Wardell. "You still have the New Line Colt?" he asked.

"You mean that little pistol you handed me back at the Huppa camp? I've got it right here. Do you want it back?''

"Keep it for a while. And keep an eye on Potter."

"Do you expect trouble from him?"

"I wouldn't put it past the guy," Clint said. "Unless I'm reading him incorrectly, Potter doesn't want to return to Talo—and I think I can guess why."

"Because he broke out of jail?"

Clint nodded. "And he and Crawley probably went through Sheriff Sloan when they escaped."

"Good Lord!" the Briton rasped. "Do you think they killed him?''

"I think it's a good possibility."

"Shouldn't we take him back to Talo to stand trial?''

"I'm in favor of that," the Gunsmith answered. "But Potter won't feel the same way. If he knows a noose is waiting for him in Talo, he won't mind killing us to avoid going back there. I might have to turn my back on him and he might decide to smash my head in with a rock when I do. That's why I want you to keep an eye on him as well.''

"Very well, Clint," Wardell agreed. "But I'm not much with a gun, you know."

"You won't have to be. Potter doesn't have a gun and he isn't aware you're armed. Luckily, taking him back to Talo will be easy enough, thanks to the mobile jail cell you brought in the back of your wagon."

"The sasquatch cage!" Wardell smiled. "It will certainly hold Potter. I never dreamed we'd lock a human being in that thing, but I suppose since we hauled the cage out here we may as well make use of it."

"Potter might feel otherwise." Clint grinned.

They climbed along the rim of the ravine and moved to the treeline. The wagon and horses had been left in a clearing within the forest. As they approached, the Gunsmith and his group saw the shape of the buckboard with the big steel cage bolted to the back of the rig.

"Good." Janice sighed. "It's still here. I hope the food supply is intact. I'm so hungry the weeds are beginning to remind me of a salad."

"There's also a keg of coal oil in our gear," Wardell added. "It'll be easier to keep our torches burning with it. We'll also have the lanterns to help us get out of this bloody wilderness."

"Doctor!" Janice laughed. "Your language!"

The Gunsmith didn't feel as optimistic as his companions. A gut instinct told him something was wrong. As they reached the clearing, his fears were confirmed.

The horses of the Wardell wagon lay sprawled on the ground, still hitched to the rig. Clint stepped into the clearing, his Parker-Hale held ready. A large dark lump lay near the wagon. Koduc's Mule.

"What in hell happened to them critters?" Potter wondered aloud.

Janice rushed to the team horses and knelt beside the motionless animals. The expression on her face, bathed in torch light, was grim.

"They're dead," she announced. "Their necks have been broken."

"What?" Potter began, stunned. "What could be strong enough to bust a hoss's neck . . ."

He realized how unnecessary the question was even as he asked it. Everyone present knew the answer.

And if anyone had any doubts, at that moment a terrible bestial wail filled the forest.

The cry of the sasquatch.

# TWENTY-EIGHT

"Jesus," Clint whispered, awestruck by the newest twist of fate. "That goddamn monster got here ahead of us. The son of a bitch *knew* where we were heading!"

"Astonishing," Wardell added. "Its intelligence must be very close to human to plan something like this."

"So is its desire for revenge," the Gunsmith remarked.

Then a terrible realization hit Clint with the impact of a rifle butt to the belly. He glanced about for Duke. The big black gelding wasn't there.

"Duke!" he shouted. Clint whistled and waited for the horse to reply. "Duke!"

"Damn it, Adams!" Potter spat. "Don't holler like that! You'll attract that big hairy bastard for sure!"

"If it killed Duke, I'll hunt that Bigfoot down," the Gunsmith hissed in a hard, cold voice. "I'll cut its balls off before I kill it!"

"Sure you will." The bounty hunter snorted. "How about us concentratin' on staying alive? If you want'a go after Bigfoot with just a bowie knife, gimme your guns before you leave."

"Shut up, Potter," Clint warned. "You've been nothing but trouble for us from the start—"

"Let's not quarrel among ourselves," Janice urged.

"She's right," Wardell added. "We have the sasquatch to worry about. Isn't that enough?"

"Yeah," Potter agreed. "And that thing is out there just waiting for us."

"Not *just* waiting," Clint corrected. "It's planning to attack us."

"Now, we don't know that," Wardell said. "It tracked us, true, but it couldn't have realized this camp is ours. . . ."

"Why did it kill the horses?" Janice wondered. "It didn't eat their flesh and they certainly didn't attack it. Why?"

"Maybe it's just so crazy with pain it's ready to kill anything," Clint said. "Or maybe it killed the horses so it could trap us here for its final revenge. I don't know. We can't climb inside the Bigfoot's head, but I still think it's going to attack us and we'd better get ready for it."

"Shit, Adams," Potter scoffed. "How do you get ready to fight a monster like that?"

"Well, we'll all pass out from malnutrition if we don't get something to eat," Janice declared as she climbed into the back of the wagon.

"Would you pass me the lanterns, dear?" Wardell asked as he approached the rig.

The girl lowered the lamps over the side to Wardell. Clint walked to Koduc's dead mule. Potter followed the Gunsmith, still holding a torch in his fist.

"You ain't that hungry, are you, Adams?" The bounty hunter chuckled.

"Hardly," Clint replied. "There are a couple blankets pinned under this mule. We might need them. Besides, Koduc's knapsack might be under there too."

"You reckon to find some sorta Huppa magic charm to ward off the *O-Mah*?" Potter snickered.

"No, but Koduc had a bottle of red-eye. I don't know about you, but I could sure use a slug of whiskey right now. Even rotgut."

"Hell, yes!" the bounty man agreed.

"Janice?" Wardell called. "I'll need the coal oil to fill these lanterns."

"Here you are, Doctor," she stated, hauling the keg over the side to the Englishman.

"Thank you, dear," he said. "What's for dinner?"

"Whatever we can fix quickly," Janice told him.

"Hey, Adams," Potter began, "if you can pry this dead jackass up an inch or two from the ground, I'll try to reach under him and see if'n that knapsack is there."

"Okay," Clint said. "If it is, I hope that bottle isn't broken."

He pushed the buttstock of the Parker-Hale under the mule. Using the rifle for a lever, he slowly pried at the dead animal until it raised slightly. Potter got on his knees and stuck his torch in the ground as he tried to slip a hand under the mule.

"Come on, Adams," he complained. "Lift this moth-eaten critter, damn it!"

"I'm not going to break this rifle stock for a lousy bottle of whiskey," Clint told him. "Let's get a tree limb and a rock to use for a lever and fulcrum."

"Goddamn whiskey probably ain't under this jackass no ways," Potter growled.

"If you don't like the service, find another saloon."

"You're about as funny as an ax killer me and Mike tracked down in Utah a few years a—"

A sudden bestial roar interrupted Potter. Clint yanked the rifle stock out from under the mule as he desperately scanned the area for the sasquatch. Potter grabbed his torch and scrambled upright.

"Jesus!" he exclaimed. "Where is the bastard?"

Then Janice screamed.

Clint turned and saw the wagon tip sideways. Wardell was still kneeling beside the rig with the lanterns and keg of coal oil. He cried out in terror as the wagon fell toward him.

Janice jumped from the rig and landed in an awkward roll across the ground. The vehicle crashed to earth a split second later. Wardell screamed when the iron cage smashed down on him.

"Son of a bitch!" Clint shouted as he bolted to the wagon, the Parker-Hale braced against his hip.

A huge, bulky shape moved along the length of the overturned wagon. The hideous, savage face of the sasquatch appeared above the edge of the rig for an instant. The beast seemed to realize that the instrument in Clint's hands was a weapon. It crouched low behind the vehicle.

"Kill it, Adams!" Potter cried.

The Gunsmith dashed around the rear of the rig. He saw the creature plunge into the trees. Clint raised the rifle and gazed down its barrels. The front sight bisected the broad shaggy back of the sasquatch. Clint began to squeeze the trigger.

Then the beast moved, its unbelievable speed and strength allowing it to plow through the brush as easily as a man might pass through the batwings of a saloon.

The Gunsmith eased the pressure on the trigger. There was only one round left in the Parker-Hale. He couldn't afford to waste it.

The sasquatch had escaped once more.

# TWENTY-NINE

Janice Powers rose unsteadily to her feet as Clint Adams moved to the center of camp. She stared at the wagon and gasped when she saw Edward Wardell pinned under the heavy steel cage.

"Doctor!" Janice cried, rushing to the rig. "Doctor, can you hear me?"

"My eardrums may be the only thing that *isn't* broken," the Englishman replied with a feeble laugh.

The Gunsmith and Jake Potter joined Janice by the cage. The Briton lay on his back, his chest trapped by the steel pen. Clint smelled the strong odor of coal oil. He spotted the shattered keg lying next to Wardell.

"Get that torch away from him!" the Gunsmith told Potter. "One spark and he'll burn up faster than a pile of dry leaves in a brushfire."

"You certainly know how to reassure a chap, Clint," the Englishman remarked, wheezing hard.

"How badly do you seem to be hurt?" Janice asked.

"Quite," Wardell rasped. "I think a couple ribs are broken. Possibly a cracked sternum as well. Something feels wrong in my face. Dull, throbbing there. Difficult to describe really."

"We've got to get him out from under this cage," Clint declared.

"He's probably suffered considerable internal injuries,'' Janice warned. ''To move him could be dangerous. A broken rib or collarbone can be driven into the heart and lungs by a mere nudge. Splintered ribs are like sharp flint. If we move him, it could be fatal, Clint.''

''Damn it,'' the Gunsmith insisted, ''we can't leave him trapped under this thing!''

''How would we move it?'' Janice asked. ''The cage alone weighs almost five hundred pounds. And it's still bolted to the wagon.''

''How about we unbolt it so we'll only have to move the cage?'' Potter suggested.

''The bolts aren't going to be easy to remove,'' Clint observed. ''Besides, if we did unbolt it the entire weight of the cage would be on his chest. That would cave in his broken ribs for sure.''

''Not to mention his sternum,'' Janice added. ''Bone shards could be driven directly into his heart or esophagus.''

''Potter and I were going to use some rocks and tree limbs to lift Koduc's mule,'' Clint said. ''We'll use the same tactic here. We'll set up two levers with fulcrums and pry the cage upright at the same time. That ought to raise it high enough to allow you to pull Edward free.''

''But moving him at all could kill him,'' she insisted. ''He could have massive internal injuries, spinal damage, head wounds . . .''

''We can't ride into town and fetch the nearest doctor for him,'' Clint said. ''You seem to know more about anatomy than Potter or I, so you'll have to be his doctor, Janice. We have to take the chance and move him. The constant pressure of the cage is apt to kill Edward anyway. Sooner or later he'll start to squirm under there. A slight shift could make the broken ribs bury themselves into his lungs. It's a gamble. . . ."

"With Edward's life," Janice said sternly. "Doesn't that make a difference?"

"Yeah," Clint nodded. "It means we can't just walk away like you can if you don't like the way the cards are going at a poker table. We have two choices: Get him out from under the cage or leave him. Either way, he might die, but we have to do one or the other."

"Excuse me," Wardell said with a groan. "Do you mind if I offer my opinion on this matter? After all, you're discussing my life, you know."

"We figured you maybe passed out," Potter said sheepishly.

"I haven't been that lucky yet," the doctor replied. "My decision is that you try to lift the cage and move me. I'd rather take my chances that way than remain pinned under this thing." He managed a slight smile. "Frightfully undignified, you know."

"Okay, Edward." The Gunsmith nodded. "We'll give it a try."

"That log over yonder might do for a lever," Potter remarked.

The bounty hunter strode to the fallen tree limb while Janice opened her suitcase and found a medical emergency kit. Clint prepared to search for another lever and rocks, but Wardell called him back.

"Clint," the Englishman whispered. "I think you can reach through the bars and get to my shirt. That little pistol of yours is still tucked away there. Might as well take it now. I certainly can't use it."

"There's no hurry for that," Clint said.

"But when you move me there's a chance Potter might find it. Take it now, Clint."

"Okay," the Gunsmith agreed, reaching between

the bars to grope for the New Line Colt in the Briton's belt. He found the small pistol and removed it from the Briton's belt. Clint tucked the .22 inside his own shirt. Wardell gazed up at him and cleared his throat.

"Clint," the Englishman whispered. "If I've got a broken back or something like that . . ."

"I'll see to it you don't suffer," the Gunsmith vowed grimly, well aware what Wardell was about to ask.

"Thank you, Clint," the doctor said sincerely.

"I don't know what good anything I have here will be," Janice admitted, having inspected her first aid gear. "I've only got some ointment, bandages and such. You know, I'm just a zoologist, not a medical doctor. . . ."

"You'll have to do your best," Clint told her. "That's all any of us can ever do."

"That log ain't gonna do, Adams," Potter declared as he walked back to the wagon, holding his torch high. "It's half rotten. We'll have to find another branch. A big one."

The bellow of savage inhuman rage again vibrated through the forest. Clint swung his Parker-Hale toward the sound. Something burst from the treeline. A massive bundle of branches and pine needles suddenly lunged forward.

For a fleeting instant, a bush seemed to have uprooted itself and attacked the camp. Then Clint saw the enormous hairy figure behind the foliage which held the large tree limb. The sasquatch was using it as a battering ram.

Janice screamed as the beast charged into the camp with its monstrous lance. Potter jumped aside, barely avoiding the branches. Clint moved to a better angle for a clear shot and aimed his rifle at the snarling sasquatch.

Suddenly, the creature turned sharply and swung the tree limb. Branches swept into Potter. The blow sent the bounty hunter sprawling to the ground. Potter's torch flew from his grasp when the regulator hit the earth.

The Gunsmith got the beast's head centered in the sights of his rifle and prepared to squeeze the trigger. The sasquatch swung the limb again and the leaves distorted Clint's view once more. With a fearsome roar, the monster hurled its weapon at Clint.

Desperation and highly conditioned reflexes saved the Gunsmith. He dodged the enormous missile. Nearly losing his balance, he fell to one knee, still facing the sasquatch. The hurled limb crashed into some trees behind Clint.

Screams filled the night. Clint was vaguely aware of Janice Powers's cries and someone else's shrieks. Yet, the Gunsmith's attention remained fixed on the great hairy giant standing before him.

The beast towered above Clint, its seven and a half foot tall hirsute frame bathed in the glow of yellow firelight. The sasquatch raised its incredibly long arms. Dark eyes burned in its terrifying face as its lips curled back to reveal its big teeth and boar-tusk incisors.

Clint squeezed the trigger of his rifle.

The Parker-Hale exploded. A burst of glaring light blossomed from the barrel and the Gunsmith's arms rose with the fierce recoil of the big game gun. He actually saw the blood erupt from the center of the monster's torso when the .60 caliber slug hit the sasquatch.

A banshee cry of agony and anger bellowed from the

creature as its body hurtled backward from the impact of the bullet. It crashed to the ground, arms and legs thrashing violently. Then it rolled over, leaped to its feet and charged into the forest, still roaring in fury and pain.

"Got you that time, you bastard!"

Then he turned to see a different kind of nightmare.

The wagon was covered with flames. Janice and Potter dug and kicked dirt, shoveling it into the fire in a desperate attempt to extinguish the blaze. Doctor Edward Wardell screamed. He was still trapped under the cage. His body was cloaked in flame.

"My God!" Clint exclaimed as he dashed forward to help fight the fire.

They piled more dirt on the blaze and smothered the flames which had engulfed the Englishman. Clint's stomach turned as the evil, sweet stench of charred flesh assaulted his nostrils. Only tattered, burned rags were left of Wardell's clothing. His skin was blistered and scarred.

"Nooo!" Janice wailed, burying her face in her hands.

"Oh, Christ," the Gunsmith rasped, shaking his head.

Smoke rose from what remained of Edward Wardell. A black, eyeless skull stared up from between the bars.

# THIRTY

"I dropped the torch when that thing hit me with that tree," Jake Potter explained. "The torch landed by the wagon and set fire to the coal oil."

"It wasn't your fault," Clint Adams assured him. "It was an accident."

The bounty hunter stared down at the burnt corpse of Edward Wardell. "No man should have to die like that."

"I don't suppose we'll be able to bury him, will we?" Janice inquired, her voice a dull monotone. She refused to open herself to emotion, realizing it would overpower her.

"We can't," the Gunsmith replied. "I'm sorry."

"You're sure you hit that goddamn devil, Adams?" Potter asked.

Clint nodded. "I shot it in the stomach. The sasquatch fell, rolled and ran off into the forest."

"A sixty caliber should have brought it down for good," Potter mused. "Hell, you could kill an elephant with that gun. Why didn't it stop the Bigfoot?"

"There's a pool of blood on the ground where I shot the sasquatch," Clint told him. "It left a trail of blood when it ran into the bushes."

"But it didn't die," Potter insisted. "That thing ain't just an animal. The way it found us just ain't natural, and the way it's been whittlin' away at us, pickin' us off one by one, that's cunnin' right outta Hell.''

"It is very intelligent," Janice agreed. "Using the tree limb for a weapon proves that. Very few animals use any type of tool, you know.''

"Ain't no animal," Potter stated. "Maybe the Huppa was right. Maybe it is an evil spirit. We can't kill it!''

"The sasquatch bleeds, damn it," Clint said. "If it bleeds, it can be killed. The bastard was hurt pretty badly this time. It may be lying dead already somewhere in the forest.''

"Don't count on it," Potter growled. "Better reload that cannon of yours, Adams.''

"I can't reload it," Clint said. "I don't have any spare ammunition for the rifle.''

"What?'' The bounty hunter glared at Clint. "How could you be so stupid, Adams? You're supposed to be the great and famous Gunsmith! How could you screw up like this?''

"He didn't," Janice explained.'' Wardell gave him the rifle. The doctor didn't want the sasquatch to be shot unless there was no other choice. He thought two rounds would be enough.''

"Jesus,'' Potter whispered. "You mean we ain't got anything left to fight that monster-demon with?''

"You keep bellyaching that it can't be killed.'' Clint shrugged. "So what difference will that make?'' Potter glared at Clint. The Gunsmith ignored him. "I've still got my Colt revolver," he added. "And we can make more torches. . . .''

"What good will that do?'' Potter demanded. "Fire ain't stopped that critter so far!''

"It seems to keep its distance until it can figure out a new way to attack us," the Gunsmith replied. "That might be because we have fire."

"Where that devil comes from," Potter began, "there's fire everywhere! Hellfire that'll burn for eternity!"

"Knock it off, Potter!" Clint snapped. "One advantage we have is our intelligence, but that won't help us if we panic!"

"What do we do now, Clint?" Janice asked.

"It'll be dawn in a couple hours," he said. "We'll wait until the sun comes up before we move on."

"As dense as the forest is, that might not make a lot of difference," Potter whined. "The Bigfoot will still have plenty of cover to hide in."

"True," the Gunsmith said, "but it's seriously wounded and it won't be able to move as fast as it did before. A belly wound with a sixty cal is bound to rob even that big son of a bitch of a lot of strength and endurance."

"Especially if its abdominal aorta has been severed," Janice added.

Clint nodded, pretending he knew what the hell she was talking about. "And the beast has a pungent musky odor. A gut-shot animal smells even worse. We should be able to detect the sasquatch long before it can get close enough to attack again."

"That sounds real rosy, Adams." Potter snorted. "But don't forget the only weapon any of us got is that forty-five revolver of yours. That gun is a peashooter compared to a sixty-caliber rifle. That didn't stop the Bigfoot. Do you really think you'll do any better with a pistol?"

"If the sasquatch attacks"—the Gunsmith

shrugged—"we'll find out, won't we?"

"Damn you, Adams!" Potter spat. "Who put you in charge anyway? You ain't done so good as a leader, if'n you ask me!"

"I'm staying with Clint," Janice announced. "You can leave if you wish, Potter."

"I ain't about to wander out there on my own, and you both know it."

"Then make yourself useful," Clint told him. "Help improvise weapons in case we need them."

"Improvise?" The bounty hunter's jaw dropped. "With what?"

"One improvises with what happens to be available," Clint replied. "If all the coal oil hadn't burned up, we could make some firebombs by using the lanterns with some rags. The only thing left to do is to make some spears."

"Spears!" Potter exclaimed. "You're suggesting we can fight that giant devil with spears? You're crazy, Adams!"

"It's better than being unarmed," Janice stated. "We can sharpen points on some sticks and harden the tips in fire."

"Hell," Potter muttered. "I guess we ain't got no other choice."

They built a campfire and fed kindling into the blaze. Clint used a Stockman pocket knife to whittle points on the ends of two long, straight branches. Janice supervised the fire treatment. She held each spear in the flames for a minute at a time and then examined the tip and scraped a flat stone across it before returning it to the fire. Almost an hour later, the crude lances were complete.

Clint managed to get the horse blankets out from under Koduc's dead mule. He used the cloth to improvise knapsacks. Clint filled them with the canned goods that survived the fire and knotted the ends of the blankets together. He cut off the reins from the dead team horses and tied them to the bags to make shoulder slings.

No one felt like eating under the circumstances— with Edward Wardell's charred corpse nearby—but later, on the trail, they'd be grateful for the food and other supplies. Besides, preparing the weapons and gear kept them busy and easing tension and making them feel less helpless.

The sasquatch had not launched another attack and they had not seen or heard it moving in the forest. Perhaps the beast had finally retreated for good or perhaps it really was dead. . . .

"What was that?" Potter asked nervously as he clenched the shaft of his spear so tightly his knuckles turned white.

Clint heard it too. Something was moving among the trees. A large form rustled bushes as it advanced toward the camp. Clint peered into the forest, trying to locate the source of the sounds.

"There it is!" Janice declared, pointing at a shape among the shadows.

A big, powerful animal approached. Its muscular dark body passed through the knotted vines and bushes as easily as a man might walk through a beaded curtain.

"It's coming at us again!" Potter exclaimed.

"Don't lose your head!" Clint told him. "Get ready, but don't make a move until we've got a clear target."

The Gunsmith drew his modified .45 Colt from leather and prepared for the final showdown with the sasquatch.

# THIRTY-ONE

The beast drew closer, its form still distorted by the dense foliage which surrounded it. Clint, Janice and Potter waited. The Gunsmith felt his stomach knot into a familiar cold ball. Fear was no stranger to Clint Adams and he felt no shame for the emotion.

Only a madman is without fear in the face of danger. Fear sharpens the senses and increases adrenaline. Controlled fear makes a man more cautious and alert. Like any other emotion, fear only becomes a liability when it clouds one's reason.

The big black creature continued to advance.

Then Clint saw the familiar shape of a long, graceful neck extending from a powerful torso and topped by an oblong head. The Gunsmith whistled. A loud neigh replied.

"Duke!" Clint exclaimed. "It's Duke!"

He holstered his revolver as the great black Arabian gelding trotted eagerly from the forest and headed for Clint. The horse rubbed his muzzle into Clint's chest and the Gunsmith hugged the animal's neck.

Potter and Janice were surprised by Clint's display of emotion for his horse, but the Gunsmith ignored them. He had feared Duke had been killed by the sasquatch like the team horses and Koduc's mule, but his friend and partner had returned unharmed.

"I knew you'd be too smart for Bigfoot!" Clint told Duke. "When that hairy son of a bitch showed up, you hid in the woods and waited for me to come back, didn't you, big fella?"

Clint turned to the others, grinning like a kid on Christmas morning. "How about that?" he declared. "Duke managed to hide from the sasquatch! He played hide and seek with Bigfoot in the monster's own forest—*and won*!"

"That's great, Adams," Jake Potter muttered, rolling his eyes with disgust. "Too bad your hoss can't talk. Maybe his advice would be better than what you've been able to come up with."

"Duke is the best ally a fella can ask for," the Gunsmith stated. "Besides, there're other supplies in the saddlebags on his back and another canteen full of water."

"That hoss is plenty big," the bounty hunter remarked. "Figure he could carry three people at the same time?"

"I won't put that kind of strain on him," Clint replied, scowling at the bounty hunter for making such a suggestion. "We can take turns riding him, but we won't all pile on at once."

"Yeah," Potter said. "He's your horse."

"Don't you forget it," Clint confirmed as he patted Duke's neck.

"Bet he can run mighty fast too," the regulator added. "Providing he only has to carry one man on his back."

The Gunsmith didn't like Potter's remark. He glanced over his shoulder to see the bounty hunter raise his spear. Jake Potter aimed the lance point at Clint's back and lunged forward.

Clint pivoted fast. The thrusting tip of the spear narrowly missed the Gunsmith. Janice screamed. Duke backed away as the spear stabbed space between Clint and the horse's neck.

Potter realized his treacherous attack had failed, but he immediately followed up by shoving the shaft of his spear into Clint's chest. The blow knocked Clint off balance. He fell on his back and stared up to see the bounty hunter's lance fly toward his prone body.

The Gunsmith rolled aside and the spear struck the ground beside him. Clint quickly grabbed the shaft of Potter's lance and pulled hard. The bounty hunter's momentum was abruptly increased. He stumbled forward and Clint's legs rose to drive both feet into Potter's belly.

The bounty hunter was propelled backward by the kick. His fingers slipped off the shaft of the spear and he fell heavily to the ground. The Gunsmith tossed the lance aside and rolled to one knee. Potter began to rise. Clint drew his Colt .45 and aimed it at the regulator.

"Oh, Jesus!" Potter cried. "Don't shoot me!"

"Why not?" Clint growled. "You tried to kill me. Then you planned to steal Duke and leave Janice here to fend for herself against the sasquatch. Your plan wouldn't have worked anyway, you dumb ass. Any man climbs on Duke's back, when I'm not there to control him, would be thrown to the ground and stomped to death. Duke's a one-man horse and he takes a downright violent dislike to rude strangers."

"I sort of lost my head. . . ." Potter said, his hands held high in surrender.

"Not yet," the Gunsmith replied, aiming his pistol at the bounty hunter's face as he cocked the hammer.

"Don't, Clint!" Janice cried. "Hasn't there been

enough bloodshed already?''

"There might have to be a little more," Clint declared grimly. "That'll be up to Potter."

"I ain't gonna cause no more trouble, Adams," the bounty hunter promised.

"Yeah," the Gunsmith replied. "I'll make sure of that."

# THIRTY-TWO

"Damn you, Adams!" Jake Potter spat. "What am I gonna do if'n the Bigfoot attacks again?"

"You'll die," the Gunsmith replied.

The bounty hunter glared at him. Potter's hands were tied behind his back and his ankles were bound together. Clint Adams opened his canteen and poured water into his stetson. Duke eagerly drank from the hat while Clint gazed up at the sky which peeked between the branches overhead. The firmament was gradually growing lighter.

"It'll be dawn soon," he remarked. "We'd better get ready to move."

"Are you certain we'll be able to find our way back to Talo?" Janice asked.

"Getting out of the forest will be a lot easier than getting here was," Clint assured her. "We just have to go back the way we came. Hell, we had to hack through a couple tons of foliage on our way in. Plants don't grow fast enough to cover that kind of a path—not even in this awful place."

"Ain't you gonna cut me loose?" Potter asked.

"Sort of," the Gunsmith answered.

He opened his Stockman pocketknife and held it in his left hand as he drew the double-action Colt .45 with his right. Clint knelt beside the bounty hunter and aimed the pistol at Potter's face as he lowered the knife blade to the regulator's bound legs.

"You try to kick me, I'll blow your head off," the Gunsmith warned.

He sliced the ropes at Potter's ankles. Clint rose and holstered his pistol. The bounty hunter struggled to climb to his feet without the use of his arms.

"Ain't you gonna free my hands?" Potter demanded.

"After you tried literally to stab me in the back?" Clint shook his head. "You can't be serious, Potter."

"Look, Adams, gimme a break, okay?"

"Sure." The Gunsmith shrugged. "What would you like? A broken neck or just an arm or a leg?"

"I can't go back to Talo," Potter said. "They'll hang me if I show my face in town."

"So you and Crawley killed Sheriff Sloan when you escaped from the jailhouse," Clint commented. "That's what I figured."

"I didn't kill him—" Potter began.

"Of course not," the Gunsmith sneered. "I bet Sloan tossed you fellas the keys to your cell and then chose that moment to commit suicide. How'd he do it? Cut his own throat or shoot himself in the back?"

"Damn it!" Potter snapped. "Mike done it. It was an accident. We got Sloan to come to the cell door and then grabbed him and yanked him into the bars. Mike just rammed the law-dog's head into the iron too hard is all."

"I bet," Clint said. "Of course, Mike Crawley is dead, so he can't give his version of what happened."

"Hell, you didn't seem to care much for Sloan no ways."

"That doesn't mean I approve of killing the guy."

"Shit! We didn't mean to do it!" Potter insisted.

"Just like you didn't mean to try to shove that spear in my back, huh?" Clint muttered.

"You go to hell, Adams!" Potter snarled.

He suddenly whirled and bolted into the forest. The Gunsmith cursed under his breath and chased after the bounty hunter.

Potter thrashed his way through a cluster of bushes and jogged a hundred yards to a giant spruce. Clint found the regulator with his back pressed against the tree trunk. Potter rubbed his wrists along the rough bark to tear apart the ropes that bound them together.

"Okay, you got your morning exercise," Clint remarked, drawing his revolver. "Now, get your ass back to the camp!"

"You ain't gonna shoot me, Adams," Potter declared as he freed his arms. The regulator's hands and wrists were scraped raw and bloody.

"I won't kill you," Clint admitted. "But I wouldn't mind putting a bullet in each of your kneecaps and dragging you back with me."

"You ain't gonna take me back to Talo. Ain't no way I'm gonna hang. . . ."

A long hairy arm suddenly extended from the branches of the spruce tree above Potter. Enormous fingers seized the bounty hunter's throat. Potter's eyes bulged and his tongue jutted from his mouth as the powerful arm lifted him off the ground.

Clint watched in horror as the regulator's body convulsed in midair. His legs and arms slashed hopelessly at empty space. The Gunsmith ran closer to the tree and gazed up at the sasquatch, perched on a large thick limb.

He raised his pistol and aimed at the monstrous

shaggy figure which now held Potter's head in a murderous two-handed vise. The beast roared as its fingers ripped flesh and muscle.

Clint fired two rounds into the creature's torso. The sasquatch bellowed. Potter's body fell from the branches and landed in a seated position at the base of the tree. Blood pumped from the ragged stump of Jake Potter's neck.

The Gunsmith pumped another bullet into the great hairy beast. The creature shrieked and swung an arm. Something flew into Clint's chest and knocked him off balance. He fell on his back, whatever the creature had hurled at him rolling next to his arm.

It was Potter's head.

The beast leaped down from the spruce. Its huge body was stained scarlet with fresh blood. The large gory wound in its stomach was rimmed by pulverized, bleeding skin. Snakelike intestines jutted from the gap. Spittle and blood dripped from the creature's open jaws as it lumbered toward the Gunsmith.

"Holy shit!" Clint cried as he scrambled away from the Bigfoot and aimed his Colt at the monster's head.

Janice materialized from the bushes, her fists clenched around the shaft of a crude spear. The girl's courage was incredible. Without hesitation, she charged forward and thrust the lance into the beast's huge body.

The sasquatch howled as the wooden point pierced its side. It swung about with remarkable speed for a large and seriously wounded creature. A slashing forearm struck the spear lodged in its ribcage. The shaft snapped in two. Janice staggered away from the giant as it turned toward her.

Clint fired his Colt. The sasquatch's head jerked as a

.45 caliber bullet smashed into the side of its skull.

The beast half turned to face Clint. The Gunsmith squeezed the trigger of his Colt again. The sasquatch's left eye exploded from its socket, crimson streaking down its cheek. The Bigfoot roared and stumbled toward Clint.

*Last shot*, Clint realized. *Make it good!*

He aimed carefully, holding the gun in both hands. He cocked the hammer and fired. A bullet hole appeared between the monster's eyes. The sasquatch took another step forward and fell. The earth trembled from the impact of the gigantic body crashing to the ground.

"Clint!" Janice cried as she flung herself into his arms. "Oh, God, Clint!"

"It's okay," he assured her, embracing the girl. "It's over, Janice. It's finally over."

But then they heard a familiar half-animal, half-human wail. Another banshee voice responded to the cry from another direction. Then another beast howled.

Janice clung to Clint in terror as the Gunsmith glanced about the woods to see three huge, shaggy figures moving toward them. Clint could hardly believe his eyes. *There are more sasquatches. And we're surrounded by them.*

# THIRTY-THREE

"No!" Janice exclaimed. "No, it can't be! Not after all we've been through—"

"Stop it!" Clint snapped. "You've held up beautifully so far, don't fall apart now!"

"What are we going to do?" she sobbed.

"Come on," the Gunsmith urged, taking her arm.

He led Janice to a pair of spruce trees with large trunks set close together. It was the best defensive site readily available. They couldn't allow the sasquatches to surround them. The worst position to fight multiple opponents is to be in the middle of them. The trees offered some protection for their backs and placed tham at an angle away from the direct path of the approaching beasts. The Gunsmith scanned the branches overhead to be certain a fourth sasquatch didn't lurk among them.

Clint holstered the empty .45 revolver. There wasn't enough time to remove the spent cartridge casings and replace the chambers with fresh shells before the creatures would reach their position. He drew the New Line Colt from inside his shirt. The short-barreled .22 pistol was designed for last ditch self-defense at close quarters. How much good would it be against the forest giants? The beast Clint had killed had absorbed an incredible amount of damage before it finally fell dead. The New Line would have as much effect on a sasquatch as throwing paper wads at the creature.

Huge, hairy bodies pushed through bushes and stepped into view. Long powerful arms extended from muscular thick bodies. Massive shoulder muscles rolled beneath dense fur as the creatures walked, although their long, wide feet padded silently across the ground.

All three creatures were well over six feet tall, but none were nearly as big as the sasquatch Clint had killed. The Gunsmith found no comfort in this since he was now confronted by three of the formidable man-beasts.

The creatures turned their pointed heads slowly toward Clint and Janice. The Gunsmith held the New Line in his fist, but the tiny gun gave him little reassurance. Fighting a sasquatch with a stubby .22 was like hunting buffalo with a slingshot.

Clint examined the faces of the three beasts. Their features were broad and flat; only the dark eyes beneath sloped foreheads seemed capable of expression. The eyes were somber, without anger or malice. The beasts turned away from Clint and Janice in the jerky, quick manner of shy animals. Clint hadn't seen their faces for more than an instant, yet there didn't seem to be any menace in the sasquatchs' actions or expressions.

In fact, Clint had noticed moisture in their eyes. He couldn't be sure, but he thought at least one of them was weeping.

The Bigfoot trio shuffled to the corpse of the slain sasquatch. They stood by the body for almost a minute, grunting sounds that could have been a crude form of language. The creatures reached down and plucked at the dead sasquatch's arms and head, perhaps looking for signs of life.

Then they leaned back their heads and howled.

It was probably the most mournful sound Clint Adams had ever heard. He recalled a time in Mexico when he'd heard a woman wail in grief as she rocked her dead child in her arms. The keening of the sasquatch trio resembled that cry of utter sorrow.

The beasts—if indeed "beasts" described them—gathered up the slain member of their species. They ignored the humans as they carried their dead into the forest and continued to wail in misery.

Now the Gunsmith shared their sorrow.

It wasn't that he felt guilty for having killed the Bigfoot; there had been no other choice. But Clint did not consider it a victory. The Huppa had been right. The sasquatch had its place in the forest and it was not meant to be disturbed.

Whatever they were—a remnant of prehistoric man, a breed of ape or a race of freaks—the sasquatch were too similar to human beings to be locked in zoo cages or vivisected on laboratory tables. They were probably a dying species which deserved to live out what time was left to their kind in peace.

"I wonder if they're going to bury him," Janice Powers remarked softly.

"I really don't want to know," the Gunsmith replied.

# THIRTY-FOUR

"Well I'll be!" a voice exclaimed from a plank-walk. "It's Clint Adams and the British gal!"

The Gunsmith walked through the streets of Talo, California, with Duke's reins in his fist. Janice Powers sat on the horse's back as Clint led Duke through the town.

Clint Adams slowly turned to face the speaker. He hadn't expected to see Sheriff Sloan again since Jake Potter had confessed to killing the lawman, but the Gunsmith had been through so much over the last few days he was too damn tired to be surprised. The horror, grief, bloodshed and the grueling struggle to survive from one hour to the next had drained him physically and emotionally.

Sloan strode forward. His head was bound in white bandages. The sheriff stared at Clint and the girl as if they had risen from a graveyard. Indeed, they were a pitiful pair. Their clothes were torn and filthy. They were thin and haggard, their eyes bloodshot and red-rimmed from lack of sleep.

"Jesus," Sloan whispered. "What happened to you out there?"

"Dr. Wardell and Koduc are dead," Clint replied in a weary voice.

"Holy damn!" Sloan gasped. "Beg your pardon for my language, ma'am."

"That's all right, Sheriff," Janice assured him. She didn't even bother to look at the lawman. It would take too much effort to turn her head to face him.

"Was it those bounty hunters who killed them?" Sloan asked. "They busted outta my jail after you left. Banged my head against the bars so hard they damn near cracked my skull open. Folks said the regulators headed north after they busted out—same direction you went to go hunt for Bigfoot."

"We sort of had a run-in with the bounty hunters," Clint replied.

"They killed the Englishman and the Injun?"

The Gunsmith nodded.

"Bastards!" Sloan snarled. "Sorry 'bout my language again, ma'am."

"Potter and Crawley are dead too," Clint explained.

"You kill 'em, Adams?" Sloan smiled.

The Gunsmith sighed. "We had a pretty rough time back there, Sheriff. A couple of friends were killed, Dr. Wardell's wagon was burned and a few other things happened that we'd just as soon forget about. We left the bodies out there. If you want to go look for them, be my guest, but don't ask me to go with you."

"Reckon your word'll do, Adams." The sheriff shrugged. "Don't think I wanta go into that forest. Folks 'round here sort of figure it's a good place to leave be."

"They're right," Clint agreed as he led Duke and Janice past the lawman and continued down the street.

"Hey, Adams!" Sloan laughed. "Did you find that Bigfoot critter you were looking for?"

The Gunsmith and Janice Powers didn't bother to reply.

# AUTHOR'S NOTE

The legend of the "Sasquatch" or "Bigfoot" is a little known part of the American West. Modern tales of "Abominable Snowmen" in the United States are usually dismissed as fraud or hysteria. Yet many Indian tribes in the U.S. and Canada believed in these "forest giants" centuries ago. Some still do.

In his book *Wilderness Hunter*, Theodore Roosevelt recalled meeting a hunter who claimed his partner had been killed by a hairy man-beast in the early 1800s. *The Daily British Colonist* printed a story in 1884 which claimed a gorillalike creature had been captured in British Columbia and held in a Canadian zoo. Unfortunately, no follow-up story was printed and the fate of this sasquatch remains a mystery. There are other tales of these alleged creatures, too numerous to mention here.

Of course, this book is a work of fiction, written to entertain the reader, and the author does not claim there is any truth to the Bigfoot stories, past or present. . . .

However, most legends are based on fact.

*J.R. Roberts*

# J. R. ROBERTS
# THE GUNSMITH

## SERIES

- ☐ 30856-2 THE GUNSMITH #1: MACKLIN'S WOMEN $2.25
- ☐ 30857-0 THE GUNSMITH #2: THE CHINESE GUNMEN $2.25
- ☐ 30858-9 THE GUNSMITH #3: THE WOMAN HUNT $2.25
- ☐ 30859-7 THE GUNSMITH #4: THE GUNS OF ABILENE $2.25
- ☐ 30860-0 THE GUNSMITH #5: THREE GUNS FOR GLORY $2.25
- ☐ 30861-9 THE GUNSMITH #6: LEADTOWN $2.25
- ☐ 30862-7 THE GUNSMITH #7: THE LONGHORN WAR $2.25
- ☐ 30863-5 THE GUNSMITH #8: QUANAH'S REVENGE $2.25
- ☐ 30864-3 THE GUNSMITH #9: HEAVYWEIGHT GUN $2.25
- ☐ 30865-1 THE GUNSMITH #10: NEW ORLEANS FIRE $2.25
- ☐ 30866-X THE GUNSMITH #11: ONE-HANDED GUN $2.25
- ☐ 30867-8 THE GUNSMITH #12: THE CANADIAN PAYROLL $2.25
- ☐ 30868-6 THE GUNSMITH #13: DRAW TO AN INSIDE DEATH $2.25
- ☐ 30869-4 THE GUNSMITH #14: DEAD MAN'S HAND $2.25
- ☐ 30872-4 THE GUNSMITH #15: BANDIT GOLD $2.25
- ☐ 30886-4 THE GUNSMITH #16: BUCKSKINS AND SIX-GUNS $2.25
- ☐ 30887-2 THE GUNSMITH #17: SILVER WAR $2.25
- ☐ 30889-9 THE GUNSMITH #18: HIGH NOON AT LANCASTER $2.25
- ☐ 30890-2 THE GUNSMITH #19: BANDIDO BLOOD $2.25
- ☐ 30891-0 THE GUNSMITH #20: THE DODGE CITY GANG $2.25
- ☐ 30892-9 THE GUNSMITH #21: SASQUATCH HUNT $2.25

*Available at your local bookstore or return this form to:*

**CHARTER BOOKS**
*Book Mailing Service*
*P.O. Box 690, Rockville Centre, NY 11571*

**Please send me the titles checked above. I enclose** _____
Include $1.00 for postage and handling if one book is ordered; 50¢ per book for
two or more. California, Illinois, New York and Tennessee residents please add
sales tax.

NAME _____

ADDRESS _____

CITY _____ STATE/ZIP _____
(allow six weeks for delivery)
A1

# LONGARM

Explore the exciting Old West with
one of the men who made it wild!

| | | |
|---|---|---|
| ____ 07524-8 | LONGARM #1 | $2.50 |
| ____ 06807-1 | LONGARM ON THE BORDER #2 | $2.25 |
| ____ 06809-8 | LONGARM AND THE WENDIGO #4 | $2.25 |
| ____ 06810-1 | LONGARM IN THE INDIAN NATION #5 | $2.25 |
| ____ 06950-7 | LONGARM IN LINCOLN COUNTY #12 | $2.25 |
| ____ 06070-4 | LONGARM IN LEADVILLE #14 | $1.95 |
| ____ 06155-7 | LONGARM ON THE YELLOWSTONE #18 | $1.95 |
| ____ 06951-5 | LONGARM IN THE FOUR CORNERS #19 | $2.25 |
| ____ 06628-1 | LONGARM AND THE SHEEPHERDERS #21 | $2.25 |
| ____ 07141-2 | LONGARM AND THE GHOST DANCERS #22 | $2.25 |
| ____ 07142-0 | LONGARM AND THE TOWN TAMER #23 | $2.25 |
| ____ 07363-6 | LONGARM AND THE RAILROADERS #24 | $2.25 |
| ____ 07066-1 | LONGARM ON THE MISSION TRAIL #25 | $2.25 |
| ____ 06952-3 | LONGARM AND THE DRAGON HUNTERS #26 | $2.25 |
| ____ 07265-6 | LONGARM AND THE RURALES #27 | $2.25 |
| ____ 06629-X | LONGARM ON THE HUMBOLDT #28 | $2.25 |
| ____ 07067-X | LONGARM ON THE BIG MUDDY #29 | $2.25 |
| ____ 06581-1 | LONGARM SOUTH OF THE GILA #30 | $2.25 |
| ____ 06580-3 | LONGARM IN NORTHFIELD #31 | $2.25 |
| ____ 06582-X | LONGARM AND THE GOLDEN LADY #32 | $2.25 |

Available at your local bookstore or return this form to:

**JOVE**
*Book Mailing Service*
*P.O. Box 690, Rockville Centre, NY 11571*

Please send me the titles checked above. I enclose _____
Include $1.00 for postage and handling if one book is ordered; 50¢ per book for
two or more. California, Illinois, New York and Tennessee residents please add
sales tax.

NAME _____

ADDRESS _____

CITY _____ STATE/ZIP _____

(allow six weeks for delivery)